THE BILLIONAIRE'S GUIDE TO THE MARRIAGE DEAL

A ROMANTIC COMEDY

PIPER MARLOWE

ROMCOMS BY PIPER MARLOWE

The Billionaire's Guide to the Marriage Deal

Phoebe isn't exactly my type, which is the plan--easy to marry, easy to leave.

Some would call it a marriage of convenience. So why can't I stop imagining something more real with my fake wife?

The Playboy's Guide to the Fake Fiancée

How did all six feet of me wind up stuffed into the passenger seat of a subcompact with the nuttiest, sexiest woman I've ever met?

This fake relationship is starting to feel realer than anything I left in New York.

The Alphahole's Guide to Marrying Your Enemy

I wouldn't date Sydney Taylor if she was the last woman on earth, which is why—if I marry her—my mother will believe it's real.

After a hate-boink or two...I'm definitely going to walk away. Really.

CHAPTER 1

EASTON

You know what's really irritating?

Realizing a bee is stuck in your jock strap as you're stepping up to the plate.

Very irritating.

Tying a girl to the bedpost with an Hermes tie and forgetting it when you leave in the morning. Irritating and also annoying.

But making a presentation to the board of directors, describing why the Taylor Corporation needs to get with the 21st century and how they—*we*—should do it, only to have your own grandmother murder you in front of the entire room and step over your dead body to state that nothing's changing?

There isn't a word in the English language strong enough to describe this feeling.

Even two hours later, I step out of the glass and gold

elevators of Murray Loft with an angry black squiggle over my head, stride across the plush velvet carpet, and throw myself into the corner booth like I want to break it.

As usual, I'm the first to arrive, because my two closest friends are degenerates.

That's usually not a big deal, but today? It's annoying.

Growing up in Manhattan and spending most of my adulthood in loft after penthouse after rooftop bar with similar scenery, the view's become an old friend. The East River wants to know why I waste my time at Taylor. The increasingly infamous bridges ask if I'll ever replace my grandmother as CEO of Taylor. Closer to hand, the Chrysler and Empire State buildings have nothing to say, because a throat-clearing cough over my shoulder captures my attention.

I don't recognize the brunette at attention beside me. I thought I knew all the waitstaff here by now. Then again, I'm usually not at Murray Loft on weekdays—too busy squeezing in every hour of face time I can in the family offices in order to convince my grandmother that it's time for me to take over and listening to her tell me it's not. She thinks I'm a kid.

You'd think, given that she's nearing a hundred, she would leap at the chance for some R&R. And yet, here I am. Annoyed.

"Can I get you something to drink?" the brunette asks. Unlike most servers at this club, her voice doesn't have that cloying, faux-sweet customer service tone I've come to despise. In fact, if anything, she sounds gruff. Annoyed.

Like an actual New Yorker.

I suppress a smile. Murray Loft isn't my first choice of hang, but Dylan and Max enjoy the rich asshole vibe. This poor girl won't last long, but while she's here, the annoyance in her tone soothes mine.

"Just a Coke," I say. It *is* only noon.

She arches an eyebrow, as though she doubts my plan to stay sober until a sane drinking hour. "Sure," is her only comment before she reaches for the menu laid face-down on the table.

I catch her wrist before she can whisk it away. "I'm waiting on a couple of friends."

I shouldn't touch her. Women either hate it or drop right into my lap, and the former often gives way to the latter. But the new waitress seems immune to my charms.

She drops the menu and pulls her hand free without so much as a flush or a stammer. "Be right back with your Coke."

Then she strides across the floor—and I can't lie, it takes effort not to stare too much. She has some serious curves. I'm trying to work out the mechanics of that— does she work out to get her ass that tight, or is it a genetics thing?—when a hand waves in front of my eyes. Two familiar barking laughs ring out in unison.

"You have got to stop being such a creep," Dylan chides. He drops into the seat across from me.

Max nudges his shoulder until Dylan slides over,

then he joins him. "Nothing wrong with appreciating the view," he says, and he definitely doesn't mean the window.

I shake my head and shove the menu toward them. "What kept you two?"

"The usual," Max replies. "Hangover, oversleeping..."

"The complete lack of Ubers in Williamsburg," Dylan complains.

"We told you to avoid *Brooklyn*," Max and I tell him in unison, prompting disgruntled protests from Dylan.

"We get it," I interrupt, before Dylan can launch into a way too detailed description of some outer borough gastro pub. "Craft beer, nitro coffee, hipster paradise, blah blah."

"You two are worse than my parents," Dylan grumbles.

"I'm still surprised your mother didn't show up to sabotage your closing on that apartment." Max smirks. Then he catches my expression.

Damn it. Sometimes I really wish Max were less perceptive. More like the stereotypical bro he appears to be, someone who doesn't notice anyone else's emotions. But unfortunately, he's too good a salesman not to pick up on every feeling in the room.

"Speaking of controlling relatives, how'd it go with the Baba Yaga today?"

Max would never call my grandmother that to her face. Nobody sane would, unless they had a death wish. But while Grandma Sofia may not be a bird-legged witch living in the wilderness and devouring anyone foolish enough to cross her, she *does* enjoy crushing business opponents beneath her designer spike heels.

That, and she has retained her thick Hungarian accent all her life, despite having lived in New York four times as long as she was ever in her homeland. Sometimes I think she does it on purpose—it comes on extra-thick anytime she's talking to the few rival companies' CEOs with known xenophobic tendencies.

Today, unfortunately, she turned that formidable attitude on me.

"Well…" I hedge.

I'm spared for the moment when the waitress returns to set down my Coke. I tune out her and the guys, glaring out the window instead. From here, I can *just* make out the glass-tinted office building that houses Taylor Corporation. Only the very edge of our logo is visible, a curling *T* that, as legend has it, my grandmother crafted in our first headquarters—a windowless, bathroomless garage space she and my grandfather rented in the Bronx for $500 a month.

Today that exact same garage, probably still sans windows or a non-shared toilet, probably rents in the neighborhood of $1500.

Our family has come a long way since then. My grandparents made good on their promise to build a future for every generation to come. Unfortunately, Grandma Sofia isn't ready to trust said generation with the reins yet.

Orders finished, I can only hope they've forgotten what we were talking about, but fat chance of that.

"So," Dylan says, trying to be Mr. Casual. "Your meeting with your grandmother. She's stepping down and naming a successor."

"She will." I shrug, trying to match his level of casual.

"And let me guess." Max hones in on me again. "It ain't you."

Beside him, Dylan curses softly. "That sucks, man. Does she know about the other board members?"

"I think she found out."

Not one, but four separate board members—out of a board of only twelve trustees—have asked when I'll be stepping up. Grandma hates lies and backstabbing more than she hates tofu eggs. Her finding out would explain her delightful yet humiliating performance for those same board members. It's like a TV show.

We can't have a multibillion-dollar company relying on someone who's already had a couple of health scares: a minor stroke she'd fully recovered from and a heart murmur that led to her getting a pacemaker installed. But also because it's a new era. We have a solid hold of our usual market, but we need to expand and take advantage of new technologies and emerging areas that my grandmother still views as "newfangled flashes in the pan."

Also, I can't help but wonder if some of the board members worry I might follow in my father's footsteps. He ran away from anything to do with Taylor Corp.

Max runs a hand through his hair. "What's her excuse this time?"

I snort. "She doesn't believe I'm settled enough to

make reasonable, stable plans for the company. In front of everyone, she suggested I think about the future of the business when I could think clearly about my own future by, oh, you know, finding a wife and making her some great-grandkids."

Dylan groans. "*Why* is she so obsessed with your love life?"

"I mean, I get it."

I think about her and Grandpa holed up in that tiny apartment. Even then, broke and struggling to build the business that would one day make them rich, they didn't hesitate. They got pregnant with my aunt Sarah right after they arrived in New York. Aunts Mary, Beth, and Clarissa soon followed.

All of them, except for Aunt Clarissa, passed away too young to have kids of their own. And then Grandpa passed too, ten years ago this month.

"She wants to make sure her legacy will carry on. Not to mention she and my grandfather had this great relationship. I know she wants me to be happy, it's just..." I gesture, irritated. "It's not like I can wave my hand and make some dream girl materialize. You can't force that stuff."

Dylan nods, clearly sympathetic.

Max, on the other hand, tilts his head. "What if you could?"

I raise an eyebrow. "What?"

"I mean, Grandma wants you settled before she hands you the company. So... what if you settle?" He holds up a hand to stave off my sarcastic remark. "It doesn't have to be real. You've got enough money to buy anything you need."

"A wife isn't a thing though," I point out. "Can't just stroll down to Wives-R-Us and—"

"You know what I mean." Max waves. "Like a… what's it called? Marriage of convenience. Draw up a contract with terms, y'know? You pay her some amount, she fake marries you for however long it'd take to convince your grandmother it's legit, yadda yadda. You just need to find someone suitable."

"Define *suitable*," Dylan interjects. "Because like… you don't want to fake marry a call girl or something. Right?"

"Nothing wrong with call girls." Max shrugs. "Probably be the easiest type to convince too."

"Pretty sure my grandmother's been around the block enough times to recognize a sham when she sees one."

Dylan points at me in agreement. "Besides, seems to me like only someone shady would sign on for this. Would a contract like that *really* hold up in court if some girl comes after you with prenup lawsuits?"

"Okay, so you just find some nice girl who's down on her luck. It doesn't have to be skeezy. You'd both be helping each other out."

Max actually seems serious. I thought he was joking.

I roll my eyes. "Sounds about as easy as finding a needle in Central Park." Then I catch myself. "Actually, harder than that."

The brunette returns with more drinks: vodka club

for Max and a beer for Dylan. Again, she gives me that judgy once-over. "Anything else?"

I smirk. It's kind of amusing how she thinks she's got me pegged. Like I'm the type to slack at lunch. "Water actually."

Both her eyebrows go up now. "Okay," she says, drawing out each syllable. Then she disappears into the growing lunchtime crowd.

When I turn back to my friends, they're exchanging grins that put me on my guard.

"What?" I mutter, dreading the reply.

"What about *her*?" Max thumbs after the waitress.

I lean around him for another look, just for an excuse to check out that seemingly impossible narrow hourglass again. Then I shrug. "Not my type."

"She doesn't need to be your type, it's fake," Max says, at the same time that Dylan interjects, "Why not?"

I gesture at her. "She's too..."

She stops to take another table's order, hip cocked, one hand resting on it.

"Real," I say, then hear myself. I shake my head. "I mean, look at her. She's the salt-of-the-earth hard-working type. Probably born in *Queens*."

"For someone who isn't your type, you sure have noticed a lot about her in the last, what, five minutes you've been ogling her?" Dylan points out.

I turn my glare on him. "*Et tu, Brute?*"

"Does that mean, 'Yes, Dylan, you're right again,' in Latin?"

"She's too wholesome." There. That's what I mean.

Wholesomely fuckable, comments the other half of my brain. The part that can't help but wonder what those curves would look like without the cumbersome uniform slacks and polo shirt.

Somehow though, I can't picture her as the type of girl who'd let me tie her spreadeagled on my bed. *That's* my type.

"Perfect then." Max grins as though I've made his point for him. "You ain't in this for fun, Easton. If she gets attached, it'd only complicate things. You want someone who needs the cash, but who will *want* to walk away from the gig after her contract's up. Not some poor innocent waif desperate enough to fall for you."

I lift an eyebrow. "Only desperate girls would fall for me? You remember Sharon or—"

"Exactly right," Dylan interrupts. "You can't be sure she wouldn't. Even if you find that needle in Central Park, it's gonna be pretty difficult to thread."

But Max knocks back his vodka club with a wicked grin. Then he rounds on Dylan. "Want to bet?"

"You can't be serious," I protest. Then I notice Dylan tapping his chin thoughtfully, and I glower at him too. "I thought you were on my side."

"I am." Dylan's smile turns almost as wicked as Max's. "Ben Franklin says this ends in absolute disaster. Either she gets way too attached or turns out to be a scam artist."

Max shakes his head. "You only get to pick one disaster. And c'mon, a single Benjamin? Make it interesting, Moore."

"How about *no* disasters," I grumble, but they're ignoring me.

I should've known. They're both suckers for a gamble. It's how Max makes so much money at the hedge fund he manages and how Dylan scores so many models a million miles out of his league.

"Okay, door number one." Dylan pulls out his wallet to lay money on the table. "Five Franklins."

"Neither of you are getting paid, because I'm not—"

Before I can finish my sentence, Max sticks a hand in the air and waves. "Miss? Can you come over here for a second?"

Christ.

Even all the way across the clubhouse, I can see her eyes narrow at the gesture. I don't blame her. But she gamely scoops up the water I asked for and approaches.

"You gentlemen need something else?" she asks, setting the glass down beside me. Her eyes find mine, and I flash an apologetic grimace.

"What's your name?" Max recaptures her attention.

The wary expression never leaves her face. Clearly she thinks we're about to complain to a manager or something. "Phoebe."

"Phoebe." Max turns on the thousand-watt smile his Midwestern family all share. "My friend here will give you five grand to have lunch with him."

Under the table, I kick him in the shin. To his credit, that smile doesn't even waver.

Phoebe narrows her eyes. "Why?"

"Why not?" Max shrugs.

"For starters, because I'm not a prostitute." She turns back to me, her gaze shifting in the type of once-over I'm more accustomed to giving than receiving. "And he's not so hideous he'd need to pay a woman for a lunch date."

My eyebrows rise. *Did she just refer to me as only mildly hideous?*

"So, I'm assuming the issue is terrible social skills. Still, five thousand seems excessive. Just hire a life coach, bud." She settles her tray under her arm. "Pretty sure that would cost a lot less." Then she tilts her head. "Although, I did serve a whole table of them here last week, so maybe they charge more than I think..."

"Told you," Dylan murmurs to Max.

I need to pull this out of the fire. Otherwise, she's going to think I really am some socially incompetent psycho—or worse, that I was actually trying to buy sex.

"Just lunch," I promise. "Nothing a prostitute would do."

She arches a brow. "Prostitutes don't eat lunch?"

The assholes I call friends burst into laughter. Even I gotta fight to suppress a grin. Okay. So she's funny. That's a start. *A start to what? This is a terrible idea, remember?*

I suppress my inner critic. "An hour of your time. Five thousand dollars. I'll write the check in advance if it makes you feel better."

Suddenly, a look of understanding dawns on her face. "Is this an MLM?"

"MLM?" What the hell is that? I thought I knew all

the major kinks. Is she into something even *I* haven't heard of?

Promising, whispers the side of me I definitely should not be listening to right now. The side that can't help noting the way she's standing, hip cocked to one side, and how it accentuates the curve of her narrow waist and makes her ass jut out even farther in those grotesque uniform slacks.

Never thought I'd appreciate a uniform, but damn.

"You know, one of those multi-level marketing schemes. You recruit me to sell fancy face serums, but first I have to spend the five grand you give me on buying a million myself, and then I have to convince all my closest friends to pour their life savings into buying them from me if I want to make any profit..."

I frown. "Why would I think you need a face serum?"

She shrugs. "I don't know what you're into, big guy."

I stare. *No, she really, really doesn't.* Because it's pretty much the opposite of her. She's mouthy, suspicious, argumentative. As an actual wife, I can already tell she'd be a complete pain in the ass.

Which just might make her the needle I'm searching for. Max is right. I can't drag my usual sweet and submissive type of girl into a situation like this. I'm an asshole, but I'm not heartless. My goal is to reassure my grandmother I'm settled enough to handle the job I've been trained my whole life to do. Not wreck someone's life.

"It's just a lunch." I shrug, trying to put her at ease. "No strings attached. In public, nothing weird. I'm harmless, I swear."

"That's exactly what a serial killer would say," she points out. But she gives me another once-over anyway, a longer, lingering one. She's considering it, I can tell.

I keep my investor-charming smile plastered on, certain she'll cave. This look has never failed me yet.

But after a long moment, she leans over to pick up Max and Dylan's empty glasses. "Yeah, not happening. But feel free to leave some of that five grand as a tip if you feel so inclined."

With that, she saunters away, and I can't help but watch her go with an unfamiliar ping of disappointment. Nobody's ever actually turned down a date with me before.

It only makes me all the more certain that this woman is perfect wife material.

CHAPTER 2

PHOEBE

I lean against the bar and count out my tips. Nearby, Monty pours something into a cocktail glass and slides it my way.

"I already had my freebie for the day," I remind him.

Higher-ups here are pretty strict about the one-freebie-per-employee-per-day rules. And I think we're all aware it's meant for ordering a sandwich during your break, not downing a cocktail to deal with an especially difficult table of socialites.

Luckily, management sometimes isn't looking.

And Monty—resident bartender and also the lifesaver who got me this gig two months ago when the Jean-Georges restaurant where I'd been hostessing unexpectedly closed—nudges the drink closer. "This doesn't count. New recipe I'm experimenting with. I need taste-testing feedback to be sure it's good enough to put on next month's menu."

"Sure, that sounds likely." I smirk. Still, I take a sip anyway. No sense letting good alcohol go to waste. It's a little sweeter than I typically like, but there's a smokiness that balances it out well. "Hmm. Is there whiskey in this?" I eye the clear drink, confused.

"Mezcal. Just got a whole case from this new distillery down in Mexico trying to woo suppliers."

"I like it." I take another, longer sip, then set the drink aside and finish counting.

Today ended up being kind of slow, but what else is new on a weekday? I haven't been here long enough to earn my way onto the better nights-and-weekends shifts, so I'll take what I can get. At least I made enough to cover the rent bill coming due next Monday. And I'll be able to eat more than instant ramen.

I might, for example, be able to afford the *good* ramen.

Still, I can't help groaning. "This will not even put a *dent* in my student loans."

Monty sighs in sympathy. "Never ceases to amaze me how poorly rich people tip."

"Because they've never worked a service job in their entire lives." I rub the back of my neck and groan, then polish off the cocktail. "I don't get it. If I had that much money, I'd want to help people lower on the ladder."

"Which is exactly why you and I will never be rich." Monty grins. "We'd do something stupid like give it all away immediately."

I snort. "I did get one decent tip off table twelve."

Just thinking about my interaction with that trio of corn-fed, spoiled rich boys makes my pulse spike all over again. Okay, sure, they were hot. The guy trying to purchase a date especially so. But in that "I was raised on the healthiest fancy food money can buy and probably had plastic surgery at age twelve to make my cheekbones this sharp" kind of way. That, or his mom's a model. Dad is probably an unattractive billionaire and together they created a kid who is both attractive and rich. Yay.

Then I catch myself. *Stop being sexist, Phoebe.* For all I know, his mom could be an heiress who nabbed herself a trophy husband. Or she might be a brilliant (if unattractive) neurosurgeon who married a sexy male model.

Possibly.

Probably not though. Just, like, statistically.

Anyway, none of that changes the fact that he tried to *buy* me. Like I must be for sale because I'm working a service job? Good tipper or not, he clearly doesn't view us servers as actual human beings.

"Speaking of table twelve, you'll never believe what those guys asked me." I fish in my apron for the business card he left under his plate. It contains no name, no job title. Just a phone number and a scribble on the back. Which, for the record, is creepy. Who has cards printed up with nothing but their phone number?

Creeps and serial killers.

Again, probably. If someone were to do a study, this would probably be true.

I glance at the card before laying it on the bar in front of Monty.

In case you reconsider.

"Five thousand dollars to have lunch with one of them. The one with the dark hair, kind of broody-looking—"

Monty actually drops the shaker he's holding. Liquid spills across the bar, and he curses, grabbing a rag to mop it up. "Hold on, hold on. Table twelve, you mean..." He glances over at the now-empty booth. "*Easton Taylor?*"

I shrug. "Maxwell Anderson was the card they paid with. Don't know who's who."

Monty gestures impatiently. "Max is the square-jawed hedge fund guy. Shame he's straight by the way, he is *so* my type. No, I know exactly who you mean. I'd recognize Easton Taylor blindfolded in a packed night-club. Easton. Taylor. Offered to *pay you* to have lunch with him?"

"Why do you keep saying his name like that?" I laugh.

"Why don't you recognize it?" He swats me with the edge of his rag. "Girl, I'd go to that lunch for free, never mind in exchange for cold hard cash. Easton is the most eligible bachelor in the damn city. Richer than the cheesecake at S&S with a hefty dollop of Bezos and Gates sprinkled on top."

"Gag," I reply. "Why would I ruin a perfectly good cheesecake by adding a sprinkle of privileged rich asshole?"

Monty rolls his eyes. "I only mean his tax bracket's the same as theirs, not his personality."

"His personality can't be that fantastic, or he wouldn't need to buy a date." I scoop up my tips, hand the rest of the cash to Monty to be added to the restaurant's take, and grab my coat off the back of my chair, leaving Easton's business card on the counter.

"Hey." Monty's voice stops me. "Weren't you *just* complaining to me about tuition payments? Think about how big a dent five grand could put in those."

I pause, one hand on the back of my chair, the other still wrapped around my coat. He *does* have a point. But is paying off a chunk of my ever-increasing student debt really worth sitting through some humiliating lunch in which a Hot Rich Guy gets his rocks off on buying me? By flaunting that he's got so much money he can lure any broke girl he pleases into... okay, I suppose it's just a free meal that he's luring me into. But still.

I mean, the whole arrangement has obviously got to be sexual in nature somehow. Even if he swears he wouldn't ask me to do anything sexy. Maybe he, like, gets off on displaying control over us destitute peasantfolk or whatever.

Monty, undeterred, leans forward to catch my eye. "*Or* think about how many shifts you could afford to miss while you get started drafting your thesis. You could put that five grand toward future food and rent and not have to worry about being in here every slow day of the week."

I chew on my cheek. Just thinking about how I'm

going to balance work with my looming master's thesis is enough to send me into a mild panic attack some nights. I'm in my final year of grad school, about to graduate with a degree in clinical social work. Once I do, I can finally leave waitressing behind and concentrate on getting my degree.

CSW is hard work, but I'll be doing *real* work. Not just gambling with a bunch of stock market numbers on a screen or whatever it is this Easton guy and his friends do to make their millions.

But in order to reach my goal, and graduation, I need to write a stellar final thesis. And based on how hard it's been balancing my regular course load with work, it'll be near impossible to pull this off. Writing isn't exactly my strong suit, and my thesis advisor—who doesn't approve of the whole working-and-studying at once—has already given me repeated warnings about how much focus I'll need.

My stomach churns.

Monty's expression softens at whatever latent panic he reads on my face. "Google him. You can see if there's anything shady in the tabloids, at the very least. If this is some weird kink thing, you *know* some previous hookup of his will have spilled the beans to a gossip columnist at some point."

With a groan, I sink back onto the barstool. "Fine." I tug my cracked iPhone 7 out of my pocket.

At the sight of it, Monty makes a little *mmhmm* noise in the back of his throat that I choose to ignore. I type in *Easton Taylor* and scroll. It's definitely him all right. I'd recognize the cheekbone-to-jawline proportion anywhere. Not to mention his eyes. They look almost black in photos, but in person, there was a coyness to him. Anytime I caught his gaze, it was like he was sharing some private joke with me.

I catch myself, annoyed. *Romanticizing this creep already, Phoebe? Might as well jump into a van advertising free puppies.*

But I can't find anything shady, which, on the internet, is saying something. Instead, there's photo after photo of him at boring-looking charity dinners or business articles with a shot of him at a conference. If I click a little further and dig a little more, photos of him skiing the Alps or hiking some scenic clifftop above a beach, accompanied by various members of his handsome, square-jawed, rich dude-bro brat pack. I recognize his friends in one picture: Maxwell Anderson and Dylan Moore. Clicking on Maxwell's picture leads to a *whole* lot more scandal: breakups and flings and affairs with married women.

But Easton looks clean-cut. Suspiciously so, in fact.

I can't find any hint of him being accused of anything sordid. But really, that proves nothing. There's always a first time for sordid behavior. Thus, he might indeed have sordid intentions and has selected me as his first sordid victim.

Fine, that's a stretch.

And a lot of sordidness.

By the time I set my phone back down, Monty's smirking at me like *I told you so.*

"There's no way he doesn't have *some* skeletons in his closet," I say. "He's got to have paid someone to scrub his online presence, or like... I don't know. Blackmailed all his kinky exes into silence."

"That, or he's got the bodies buried in Jersey." Monty grins, and I snort, against my better judgment. "Look, if he actually sets off your creep-radar, don't go."

"He doesn't," I admit. "That's the problem."

"So the problem is there's no problem?"

Staring at Monty's bemused expression, I realize he has a point. Several good ones actually. Groaning, I pocket my cracked old phone. "Fine. I'll go on the date. But I'm ordering two entrees and taking one home. And if I get murdered, you're the one who has to explain it to my parents, got it?"

Monty laughs. "Deal."

"Except actually..." I think it over. "If I do get murdered and you have to explain it to my parents, could you lie? I'd hate for them to think I got murdered for believing a rich guy wanted to pay me five grand to have lunch. Make up something way better than that, would you?"

Monty is still shaking his head as I wave goodbye and take off. But by the time I score a rare seat on my normally crowded subway train home, I can't help it. I slip my phone out of my pocket and scroll through the photos again. I settle on one of Easton with his arm wrapped around a much older woman—grandmother maybe?—beaming for the cameras at some awards gala.

My gaze lingers on his smile. The genuine warmth in his eyes.

Maybe this date won't be a *complete* nightmare.

I close the search window and open a blank text. *So. I've given your suggestion some thought...*

CHAPTER 3

EASTON

I stop in the middle of the sidewalk and look up at the sign. I can't believe of every possible restaurant in the food capital of the world, this girl chose *this* place.

Phoebe looks up and flashes me a broad grin. "I'm starving! You want to go in?"

"It's... an Irish pub." I don't mean to sound like a rich asshole, but I am, so I do, and it really doesn't matter. "I figured you'd want to try some experimental popup in the East Village."

I wave my private driver, Norm, away. Keeping him on the payroll is the sort of extravagance I normally look down on. But he used to drive for my parents, and when they up and moved to Paris on a whim shortly after my father abandoned his board seat in the family business, I felt responsible. Norm was practically family. If I'd let him go, he might have ended up driving for some share-car company that horribly undercuts employees' wages and benefits.

Then I look at Phoebe, fully taking her in for the first time. Her dark curls fall loose around her shoulders, her eyes bright above angular cheekbones and full, pursed lips.

The kind of lips that would look sexy as hell wrapped around—

"MacLaren's Bar," she says, waving like she's leading me to an obvious conclusion. "Get it? From the TV show?"

"I don't watch TV," I say, dragging my gaze back up to her eyes.

Just in time to watch her roll them. "Of course you don't."

She saunters ahead of me without waiting for me to open the door for her. On the bright side, that does grant me a view of those curves of hers again. She's dressed simply—jeans and a white T-shirt. Somehow, the simplicity makes her all the more alluring. Knowing that she looks this good without even trying makes me wonder what a little effort will do.

I shake my head and jog after her. *Get it together, Taylor.*

Getting it together—apparently—means insulting her.

"I'm too busy contributing to society to stare at a screen. Try it sometime."

"It's called relaxing. You know—self-care? De-stressing makes you less of an asshole. Maybe you should try it sometime." She tosses that long hair over one shoulder when we reach the hostess stand, and she flashes a smile. "After all, you're something of a workaholic, aren't you, Easton Taylor?"

I'm confused by her use of my name until I realize the hostess is standing right beside us. I hadn't even noticed her. Too busy suppressing my irritation.

"Whatever you think you know about me—" I start, but Phoebe's way ahead of me.

She sashays after the hostess, all the while reciting over her shoulder, "Thirty-four years old, never been married or even outed as in a serious relationship by the gossip rags—which means you're either a player or a commitment-phobe. Loves travel, yacht parties, skiing, but most of all your big fancy penthouse office at your big fancy family company that gives you the money to do all the other cliché rich-bro stuff." We reach our table, and she drops into her seat with a flourish, looking far too pleased with herself. "Did I miss anything?"

"Thank you," I murmur to the hostess before I take the chair across from Phoebe.

I don't miss Phoebe's quick blink of surprise before she schools her face impassive once more.

I'm tempted to call her out for Google-stalking me. But it's not like I can talk. I spent the last few days—ever since I received her text saying she was up for this after all—checking up on her too. No criminal record, which is good, and not much of a social media presence either, which will help when it comes to avoiding tabloid exposure. The last thing I want is a million photos of my private life plastered everywhere, if I actually invite her to do this.

According to the public enrollment records NYU keeps, she's in graduate school for clinical social work, which means she's not one of those servers waiting around to get cast in *Law & Order: SVU* in the hopes of making it big either. Also a plus.

But while I've come around to a solid *maybe* on Max's ridiculous idea of finding myself a fake temporary wife, I'm not so sure I'm sold on *Phoebe* as said wife quite yet.

I pick up the trifold menu and wrinkle my nose as it just keeps expanding. At least five sections and two whole pages of desserts. Any restaurant that offers more than ten dishes to choose from is never much good.

"You missed one," I tell her. "I also pay attention to the quality of the food that goes into my body. Which means you either didn't pay attention to anything outside who I date, or you're trying to be *funny*."

"How funny? Funny ha-ha funny or funny weird funny?"

"Funny sadistic funny." Which is my role, and if there's one thing any relationship doesn't need, it's two sadists. "Because dragging me to a place whose *Recommended Bestseller* is..." I squint. "Chicken fingers with honey mustard... is cruel."

Phoebe grins, undeterred. "I hear they've also got great milkshakes."

I try not to smile, because a milkshake is a milkshake and I'm not made of stone. "Let's just cut straight to business, shall we?"

Before I can explain, however, a waiter cuts in. I watch with growing confusion as Phoebe orders half the menu: the aforementioned chicken fingers, chili cheese fries, a club sandwich, and two milkshakes. Unless she's carb-loading for an impending marathon, I have no idea where she's planning to put all of that.

"Oh, and some nachos for the table, I think." She looks up then, as though just remembering I'm here. "What're you having?"

"If your kitchen has any food leftover after serving the lady, I'll just take a burger. Medium rare." I hand the waiter my menu.

"Ha ha." She leans back in her chair, one arm flung over the back. "I'm just getting my money's worth out of whatever this is. Speaking of which…"

I sigh and reach into my pocket. I had hoped to wait at least until we got appetizers before talking cold hard cash—but perhaps it's best to be upfront. After all, this is not a date. This is a planned and paid for meeting to discuss a business deal.

But then Phoebe leans forward again, and the V-neck cut of her basic white T-shirt drops low enough to flash a tantalizing glimpse of very not-basic white lace.

Well, well. Maybe Ms. Wholesome has a naughty side.

"Five thousand dollars, as agreed." I slide her the check, facedown.

She snatches it up and scans it. The way her eyes widen and lips part faintly tells me that deep down, she didn't expect I'd actually pay up. But she manages to conceal her shock admirably well and tucks the check into her purse. "Okay, so what's your deal? Findom?"

I lean back and cross my arms, because this girl is so far off what I like, and yet kinda closer than she knows.

"That's where rich men like women who use them for their money," she continues. "I had a roommate freshman year who put herself through college stepping on guys' faces with red pumps while she called them garbage. She had this one British client she had to use the word 'rubbish' for."

"Phoebe." I arch an eyebrow. "Tell me you didn't research kinks in preparation for this lunch too."

She shrugs. "Gotta be prepared for every possible scenario."

But unless I'm imagining things, a faint hint of a blush touches her cheeks. It's enough to make my blood surge. Maybe she's naughtier than she lets on. It's enough to make me wonder what kind of kinks, exactly, get her blood rushing.

Suddenly, all too vividly, I have an image of her in my big four-poster, arms spread to either side and tied just tight enough that she can't move as I trace my mouth, my *tongue* over those luscious curves. I wonder what she tastes like. I wonder what sound she'd make when my tongue reached those soft thighs and I parted them to—

"So, would you say you tend to be a planner then? Generally speaking." I'm glad to hear my voice at least *sounds* like that of a normal interviewer, despite my suddenly racing pulse and the pressure against the seam of my work slacks. I spread my napkin over my lap and shift in the chair to conceal how stiff my cock is getting at the mere thought of touching her.

Christ. You'd think I have no self-control.

Across from me, Phoebe lights up. At first I think it's because she's finally noticed I'm interviewing her for something. Then I spot the waiter approaching with our nachos, and I roll my eyes.

She digs in eagerly, and only after swallowing two whole mouthfuls does she gulp some water and reply. "I mean, I try to plan and be organized. It's kind of hard when you're balancing work *and* grad school *and* writing a thesis though."

"I hear taking time for self-care makes you less of an asshole."

"Well, maybe I did yoga instead of making sure you're not some serial killer." She glances at me with a grin when she says this, and for some reason, I find myself suppressing a smile.

She has a certain no-nonsense charm, I'll grant her that. I tilt my head, sizing her up anew. "How do you know I'm not?"

"You've got too much 'basic rich guy' vibe."

I snort. "What, basic rich guys can't be mass murderers?"

"Nah, all the wealthy serial killers are super obvious about it. Because they know they can buy their way out if they ever get caught," she adds, gesturing with a cheese-covered chip before she slides it into her mouth and licks her fingers clean.

My gaze drifts to her fingers as she sucks each, one at

a time. *Fuck.* I grit my teeth to stop my already hardening cock from becoming a worse issue. "Like who?"

"That one real estate mogul who murdered his wife, whatshisface, from the TV series. Total psycho eyes. If he weren't rich as God, he would've been arrested *decades* sooner."

"You watch too much TV," I reply. But I'm grinning now too.

She groans. "I wish. Weren't you listening? Crazy schedule, no free time. Next semester I'm going to have to pull back-to-back all-nighters if I want to make my thesis deadline." She heaves an overdramatic sigh. "Too bad it would totally invalidate my cred as a social worker if I resorted to chemical assistance for that, am I right?"

I lift an eyebrow, which makes her burst into laughter.

"I'm *joking.* Only bucketloads of extra-strength coffee for me, thank you very much."

On paper, Phoebe makes the perfect candidate for this whole scheme. She's smart, educated, independent —but not so independent that she could afford to pass up the financial help this deal would give her. Plus, she's got goals of her own, a whole life plan, so she's not liable to get too tangled up in this arrangement. And God knows, with that mouth on her, I'm not likely to make any similar mistakes either.

Although, thinking about her mouth *does* give me several ideas about what I'd do if she ever let me tie her up and fuck her senseless.

But I'm not here to satisfy my needs. At least, not the sexual ones.

What I really need is a wife who meets my grandmother's standards. Someone who can convince Grandma Sofia to relax already, because I'm finally "settled down."

Somehow, I can't picture Phoebe convincing anyone she could settle. She's far too casual, too real, and well... *too hungry*. I watch the waiter set several plates in front of her. She sends half back to be boxed up before digging into the chicken fingers with gusto.

She catches my eye and holds one out with a grin. "Try it. I bet even food snobs like getting back to the staples sometimes."

"Basic food for a basic rich guy, I guess." I sigh, accepting the fried meat. It *does* taste better than I remember.

"When was the last time I actually ate one of these?" It's so good I don't realize I'm asking this out loud until it's out of my mouth.

"I knew it!" She's crowing, and I force my face back into a glare. Too late. She's smirking. "You like it."

"It's not the worst," I admit, leaning back in my chair.

"Neither was this," she replies, surveying the aftermath of her appetite. "As far as dates go, I've definitely been on at least four much worse ones."

"Wow, thank you." I snort.

"No, seriously." She tucks her hair behind one ear. "I'd eat with you again for like... a grand."

"Okay, that's how I know you're not a business major." I lean back in my chair and cross my arms. "You're supposed to raise your rates once you have experience at something, not drop them."

She taps her chin. "Good point. I'm selling myself short. How about a raise, boss?"

Boss. Just that word gives me visions of her on her knees, gazing up at me with those big lips pursed. Fuck. I shift in my seat. "If you're angling for a promotion, we'd have to add to your duties."

I imagine ordering her to do other things. To spread her legs and bend over this table. My cock is so hard it throbs. I swallow thickly. I'm going to have to let her leave first. Go to the restroom and wrap a fist around myself while I picture her lips closing around my shaft instead.

Phoebe actually licks her lips. Maybe she can tell what I'm thinking and she's enjoying making me sweat. But then she tsks and folds her arms, and the illusion shatters.

"I'm *still* not a prostitute, Easton."

"I never—"

"But I do appreciate your assumption that if I were, I'd at least be a high-end one." She shrugs one shoulder as her phone rings. "Hang on, there's my emergency call."

While she answers, I dig my own cell from my pocket. Five missed calls. I frown and unlock the screen. I always silence it when I'm at meals with anyone—a habit my grandmother instilled. But now, worry rises.

They're all from the office. Three from board members, and two from my assistant. Then a text arrives. Link to a *Wall Street Journal* article.

Taylor Corporation stocks take a nose-dive after co-founder and current president of the board, Sofia Taylor, fails to close yet another deal with...

I'm still reading when I zone in on Phoebe saying my name.

"Easton? Confirmed, he definitely thinks I'm a prostitute."

"I do not," I grumble, eyes still on the article.

Shit. This is exactly what I feared. My grandmother might still be a legend among entrepreneurs, but she's not the negotiator she once was. Even from this brief summary, I can picture what happened. She'll have stormed into the meeting guns blazing, without taking the time to pause and consider the intricacies of the situation.

I need to convince her to step down *now*. Before she makes any more mistakes like this. Not just for my sake, or even the company's. I know how much my grandmother, much as she'd hate to admit it, cherishes her reputation. I don't want to see it damaged just because she's loath to let go, now that the time has come.

Phoebe's still whispering on the phone, running down a list of kinks now. "He claims it's not fin-dom, so maybe a rejection fetish? Is that a thing?"

Christ almighty.

With a resigned sigh, I pocket my phone and spread my hands on the table. Fine. Phoebe may not be the *perfect* fake wife. But she's here, and that's several steps farther than I've gotten with any other potential women.

Actually, I have no other potential women, so... bird in hand and all that.

"Actually, Miss Jones, I do have a proposition for you," I say loudly enough to interrupt her conversation.

She pauses, eyes wide. "I'm gonna have to call you back, Monty." She hangs up, smirking as though she's just won something, and leans across the table. "What is it?"

"You're agreeing to an NDA before I say another word."

"I knew it. Okay, I agree. Just tell me, which kink is it?"

"Actually... it's more of a proposal."

CHAPTER 4

PHOEBE

I'm not one of those girls who daydreams about proposals and weddings. I never was. I mean, I suppose when I was younger I liked to marry my Barbies off as much as the next girl, but I wasn't fixated by it. And now, sitting in a tragically un-hip restaurant, already bloated from extra cheesy nachos and fried chicken, swearing I won't reveal the fetishes of the guy who paid me to be here, is not the way *anyone* imagines a *proposal* is going to happen.

"I need you to marry me."

Yup. That's what Ken said to Barbie, but this feels a little less romantic.

I tuck my phone into my back pocket and lean forward on both elbows, locking eyes with Easton. "Come again?"

He arches a brow. "You first."

I roll my eyes. I *refuse* to laugh at that. But I think he can tell I'm suppressing it, because his gaze darts to my mouth, and his grin widens.

"Seriously. Are you into roleplaying marriage vows or something?" I press. "Because that's... surprisingly tame."

There's a quick flicker of heat in his gaze then. The glimpse of a more intense person underneath all the casual rich boy glam makes my heart beat a little faster, my spine straightening almost imperceptibly. It's like there's another Easton underneath the one I'm seeing, a more intense, *hungrier* version.

Not gonna lie. Part of me might like to see that Easton come out to play.

But a bigger part of me knows that would be a terrible idea. This lunch in and of itself already tops the list of dumb ideas—even if the check he passed over looks legit. I can still feel it burning a hole in my pocket, just itching to pad my near-empty bank account. And spending time with him hasn't been that bad. But still. Bad. Idea.

So I fold my hands on the table and ignore the fact that Easton's looking at me as though he's hungry for more than the burger he barely touched.

He sits back too and the heat dies down, that brief glimpse of the real him vanishing once more behind a curtain of the bemused upper-class guy accustomed to getting what he wants.

"I need a wife," he says. As though that explains everything. I open my mouth, but he cuts me off. "I'm willing to pay you to fake it for a while. My lawyer will draw up a contract. A legitimate contract. I'll pay for a separate law firm to review it on your behalf, just so you know I'm not trying to pull one over on you." Before I can even ask, he adds, "We can add a no prostitution clause."

"Can you?" I quirk an eyebrow, amused. I'm visualizing the call with his lawyer, asking for a fake wife contract with a no prostitution clause. This is ridiculous enough to be funny.

He shrugs, looking dead serious. "We can add to the contract whatever you need to be comfortable, sure."

I blink. He cannot be serious. I glance around, waiting for the inevitable cameras to roll out as Ashton Kutcher pops out of a side door yelling "You've been Punk'd!"

But it doesn't happen. Nothing happens.

Another glance around the restaurant reveals that nobody is paying attention to us at all. Still. This has got to be a joke. Or a really bizarre fetish. I fold my arms as I consider Easton. I might be busy, but I'm already here and playing along should be amusing at the very least. I wonder how this works? Am I supposed to squeal with excitement or play hard to get? Heh, doesn't matter. I already have the check. "How long is *a while?*"

He considers. "A year ought to do it. It's got to be a believable length of time, so..."

I don't ask believable to whom. Not really my focus right now. "What kind of payment are we talking?" I mean, if he paid $5k just for lunch...

"I'm willing to negotiate. But I think a million should be fair compensation, don't you?"

My stomach drops.

A million dollars. That's game-changer money. That's "move out my shithole apartment with the five room-mates" money. That's "pay off my student loans without even blinking and still have a ton to shift into savings while I get on my feet after school" money. That's...

Oh, fuck. This is the best fantasy I've had in months.

I manage to keep my expression neutral, barely. Or at least, I think I do. It's been a while since I've gone to one of Monty's poker nights. Who knows, I might be losing my edge. It's hard to tell, because Easton sits there with that neutral expression, like this is a standard business lunch.

Who knows? Maybe for him, it is. Maybe he pays people to do weird shit all the time.

Mentally, I run through the real reasons he could be offering this. Gay and closeted, needing a beard? But Monty's gaydar is next level, and he didn't mention anything about Easton. And I definitely was not imagining the heat in his eyes when he checked me out earlier.

So, what then? An ex he needs to stop stalking him? Weird bet he needs to win?

I force my mind back to the present. He said *willing to negotiate*, after all. A million might sound like an impossible amount of money to me, but it's chump change to a billionaire. I trill my fingernails against the table. Left hand. "Do I get to pick out the ring, and do I get to keep it after?"

He smirks, a flash of surprise covering his face. "Great question. Yes, and yes."

I purse my lips and consider the ring finger in question, looking from my hand to him and back. "And my tuition bills, at—"

"Yes."

My eyebrows rise. "Outstanding student loans from undergrad."

"Done."

Damn. This is the hottest fetish ever. I'm not sure why I never thought of it before, because I'm almost orgasmic at the mere idea of my student debt being paid off.

Except.

I think he's serious. If he's not, if this is a practical joke, it's either the cruelest or the most accurate one ever played. Like he reached into my brain and spied everything I needed before he came here to bargain.

Before I can say anything else, someone clears their throat, loud and at my elbow. I jump, expecting Ashton. Instead, it's the waiter, setting down the bulging bag full of extra food I ordered. My stomach groans just from the smell—okay, maybe I did order a bit more than I needed. But hey, gotta get my money's worth.

I chew on my lower lip, thinking. "I'm serious about the no sex thing. I'm not—"

"A prostitute. Yes, I believe we've covered that." He smirks. "Is this you agreeing?"

"This is me thinking," I reply.

"What's there to think about? It's a straightforward offer."

There's got to be a catch—there's *always* a catch. But I'm too full of nachos and chicken tenders to reason clearly.

I stare at my takeout bags. If I walk away right now, I got five grand, three solid meals, and a hilarious story to share with Monty. On the other hand, if I call his bluff, I could have an even *more* hilarious story to share with Monty. Not to mention the off chance that Easton's actually serious about this.

I glance outside at the sidewalk, the normal New Yorkers trudging past. Most people would leap at this chance, even if it did turn out to be a scam, right?

Then I notice something. A familiar turquoise blue awning. And I grin.

"Oh look, a Tiffany's. The universe clearly wants me to say yes." I stand, grabbing my takeout. "Let's do this then."

Easton wipes his mouth and stands, looking less than enthused. "Are you serious?"

"*Ha.*" I wag a finger in his face. "I knew you were bluffing."

He catches my hand and I try to ignore the sudden heat his touch brings, the sparks that rocket up my arm. It's just all this adrenaline. Too much nacho cheese. That's it.

"I'm not *bluffing*, I just... *Tiffany's*? Really?" His nose wrinkles.

I jerk my hand from his and start for the door, leaving him to jog after me. "What's wrong with Tiffany's?"

"It's pretty much the Walmart of fine jewelers."

I scoff. "You are such a snob."

"I'm not a *snob*, I just have good *taste*."

I shove through the doors of the restaurant and into the bustle of New York. Car horns, tourists who have no idea how to follow sidewalk traffic patterns, several cursing construction workers. The sounds of home. And across the street, that Tiffany blue beckons.

"If it's good enough for Audrey Hepburn, it's good enough for me," I inform him, in a tone that brooks no room for disagreement.

He rolls his eyes. Then curses when I jump onto the street, dodging traffic to hurry across without bothering to head to a crosswalk.

"Do you have a death wish?" he yells by the time he joins me on the far side.

"What, you don't jaywalk?" I eye him sideways. "Are you even a New Yorker?"

"*Yes*. One who follows the traffic laws."

I wave dismissively. "As long as you make eye contact with the cab drivers, they won't run you over."

He's still sputtering when I glide through the door of Tiffany's.

The saleswoman at the counter gives me a once-over, quickly taking in my obviously two-for-one plain white tee and bargain basement jeans. I'm sure my bag of leftovers from a tourist restaurant confirms her estimate of my purchasing power at about a hundred bucks. But her face clears the instant Easton steps up to the counter behind me.

"What can I do for you?" she asks in a voice that clearly tells me she knows exactly who he is. And she knows damn well his purchasing power is unlimited.

Game time.

"We're looking for an engagement ring." I smile widely, bat my eyelashes in that *yeah, you misjudged me, didn't you?* look I always wanted to reenact from *Pretty Woman*. Minus the prostitution part, clearly.

The woman's eyes widen, but it's more *hell yeah, commission* than *oh sorry, obviously broke girl*. But I forgive her when she leads us to a counter toward the back and pulls out trays with some of the biggest diamonds I've ever seen in my life. Both on television and in real life.

"What do you think?" I ask Easton, reaching for the nearest one, a single stone cut in a square. It reminds me of the costume jewelry my mom used to buy me as a kid. Only this one's no costume.

"Whatever you like," he replies in a tone that suggests he's still being snobby.

Out of sheer spite, I stick it on my finger. This is a mistake. "Ow." I twist, unable to get the ring back off.

The saleswoman flutters around nervously. "Here, let me try."

I give her my hand, firing a glare over my shoulder at Easton. "It's all that salt from lunch—wouldn't you know, he pops the question out of nowhere right after we share a full course of appetizers?"

"*Share?*" Easton murmurs.

The saleswoman doesn't notice, just clucks her tongue sympathetically. "Well, we can have this sized, of course."

I eyeball the ring. Now that it's on my finger, the gem is only about the size of my pinkie nail. "Hmm, yes, speaking of size. I'm thinking this rock could use a little extra sodium too. Maybe double this?"

The saleswoman finally manages to extricate my hand from the ring. She looks from me to Easton to the tray and back. "Let me see what we have in the back."

While she disappears, I face my husband-to-be. "Well? Still serious about this?"

He crosses his arms and eyes the diamond display. "If this were a real proposal, I'd have had a custom ring made. Designed by the jeweler who does all our family's work."

"Uh huh, and what's the resale value on custom-designed rings by someone nobody on eBay has ever heard of?" I retort.

He suppresses a smile. "Ruthless."

"Is that a problem?" I tilt my head.

"No. It's why I chose *you* to do this with me."

I blink, thrown off for a second. What does *that* mean? Before I can ask, the saleswoman returns with an even bigger tray, and my smile widens in proportion.

Fifteen minutes later, we're back on the street corner, only this time I'm in danger of being blinded from the amount of sunlight reflecting off my ring. A ring that cost more than my undergrad and graduate student loans put together. So. I guess this is actually happening?

"I'll text you the details once I've got everything sorted at the courthouse," Easton says.

Behind him, the car I saw dropping him off earlier is circling around again. Does he have a *private driver?* Who am I kidding, of course he does. He probably has a gentleman of the privy to wipe his butt too, like kings in medieval times.

"Can't wait, hubby-to-be," I tell him.

There's an awkward moment where we both hover. Do we kiss goodbye? Hug? What's the proper etiquette for a man you barely know who just put a rock on your finger?

Easton holds out a hand, and I can't help but laugh, even as I place my palm in his. But when he wraps his fingers around mine, he doesn't shake. He draws me toward him a step, his fingers so hot they feel as though they might burn. He leans in to kiss my cheek, and it's softer than I expected. A slow, lingering kiss that burns all the way down my chest, my gut, into my toes.

Fuck.

"See you soon, future wife."

Then he's gone, the door of his private car slamming behind him, and I'm still standing on the street corner, breathless.

CHAPTER 5

EASTON

I pace the length of the courtroom. Turn around, pace back again.

Beside me, Max picks some lint off the lapel of his suit. "Would you calm down?"

From behind her desk, the judge eyes us all over the rim of her glasses. "Maximillian, I told you I was happy to squeeze this in as a favor to your father, but we *do* need the bride to be present for the wedding."

"What if she doesn't show?" I spin, stride back the way I came.

Dylan lounges in a chair nearby, one arm flung over the back. He's got his camera around his neck. He hasn't taken any real photographs since college, but I managed to talk him into making an exception. I'm going to need photographic evidence if I want my grandmother to buy this little scheme.

She already seemed suspicious at the office yesterday when I cornered a coworker in the kitchenette to loudly talk his ear off about the gorgeous young woman I'm falling head over heels for. I made sure to do it right at eleven o'clock, when Grandma always takes her second coffee break, so she'd be sure to overhear.

But I'd expected her to be happy for me. Or conceal a little smirk when she heard me talking. She did neither. Just harrumphed, turned on her heel, and tromped down the hall. Without her coffee.

Clearly, I need to up my game in the future.

Assuming my bride actually shows up.

"What the hell is taking her so long?" I check my watch.

The judge does the same. "I have an appointment in twenty minutes. If you need to reschedule—"

"I'm here!" Phoebe's voice cuts through the tension as the far door crashes open.

And there she is. My fake bride.

Her hair is done half-up, the rest cascading around her bare shoulders. Her eyes find mine right away, and she smiles sheepishly. "Sorry, traffic, plus I had to pick up the dress from Monty's mom's house all the way in Canarsie, so..."

To be honest, I hadn't even noticed the dress. Just her.

But now that I look at it, I have to suppress a smile. It's definitely a wedding dress, I'll give her that, but it's at least two sizes too big. It hangs away from her chest, which she only seems to notice when my gaze drops to her display of cleavage.

Damn. I knew those curves on the ground floor had an ample matching set upstairs. Plus, white lace bra. Is she planning to take the dress off at some point...?

Stop fantasizing, you ass. The no sex part of this arrangement has been made abundantly clear—even if Phoebe didn't make me amend the contract for it.

"No way I'm leaving a paper trail about my sex life," she said on the phone last night, after my lawyer had finished drawing up the contract with the few stipulations she'd bargained for—tuition payments on top of her subsidy, plus a clause about owning the ring.

Now, Phoebe claps a hand to her chest, holding the dress shut, her eyes wide. "Also, no time to get this sized, so..." She takes a step and nearly trips on the hem of her poufy train.

Over her shoulder, her friend Monty appears in the doorway. "Careful!" he scolds, snatching up the train to carry it behind her. "If I bring this back with a single spot, my mother's going to flay me, tan the hide, and make me into a sofa."

He holds the train aloft as Phoebe proceeds up the aisle of the court room, her long legs flashing under the hem, and—

Sneakers. She's wearing white leather sneakers.

She catches me watching. "What? They're real Nikes, darling."

I shake my head, but at the same time, find myself

repressing a laugh as I extend an arm to her. "Shall we, *darling?*"

Phoebe actually bats her eyelashes as she loops her arm through mine. "I've been waiting for this moment for my entire—well, last three days," she murmurs, thankfully low enough that the judge doesn't hear.

Still, I extend my elbow to nudge her side. She grins at me, unrepentant. I'm still glaring in warning when I hear the shutter of Dylan's camera. *Great.* That photo will definitely convince my grandmother we're wildly in love.

So I glare at him too, then I do my best to gaze at my bride with a besotted expression for the next photo.

Which results in difficulty. Because from this angle, even with her hand against her chest, I can see all the way down that gaping gown. Her breasts rise and fall with her breath, swells barely contained in white lace. *Fuck.* It makes me wish we were alone in this room. If we were, I'd pull her hand away. Let that gown puddle at her feet and see what else she's hiding beneath it.

Or better yet, take advantage of some strips torn off that ridiculously long hem to tie her hands behind her back, then drape her over the judge's desk and—

"Are we all present and accounted for now?" the judge's voice interrupts my train of thought. "Witnesses?"

Max steps forward, smoothing his suit again. Monty takes his place beside Phoebe, wiggling his eyebrows at her suggestively when the judge is turned.

"Please face each other and join your hands."

We do as we're told. Phoebe's hands feel cool in mine, her fingers slender, but long enough to wrap all the way around my broad palms. She peeks up at me from beneath her lashes, then winks, conspiratorial. It makes me smile again.

No, Phoebe's not my type. But maybe I've picked the right person for this charade after all, if we can enter into it and leave it as friends.

It certainly won't hurt that she's easy on the eyes. At least I won't get tired of all the lovesick gazing I'll need to do.

"Repeat after me," the judge orders. "I, Easton Malcom Taylor..."

"Malcom?" Phoebe mouths, as I repeat the words.

"... Take thee, Phoebe *Emma* Jones," I emphasize for retort when we get to her name.

"To be my lawfully wedded wife..."

More camera shutter snapping. But I'm barely listening, as Phoebe recites her part. My eyes are fixed on her lips, still quirked in that sideways smile.

"You may now kiss the bride."

We need a photo of the kiss, I know. And it needs to look convincing. But that doesn't completely explain why, when I lean in to cup her cheek in one hand, my pulse picks up. Or why, when I lean in, I do it slower than I normally would, keeping my eyes on hers until the last possible second.

She tilts her head to mirror me. I crush my mouth to hers, intending it to be quick, light. But she tastes like raspberry lip gloss, and her scent is a mix between that and a faint hint of vanilla, and I can't pull away as quickly as I'd planned.

As if reading my mind, Phoebe buries her fists in my hair and drags me closer, and my mouth parts to find her tongue already waiting.

Just for emphasis, I dip her at the waist, ignoring the faint squeal she emits against my lips as she goes tilting backward. I keep my mouth pressed to hers, but I feel the way we're both smiling. Then I tip her back onto her feet and step away, one hand clasped in hers, to the cheers of our little audience.

It's done.

The first text I get from my new wife—after spending the world's shortest honeymoon having Norm drop Phoebe off at her apartment en route back to the office—seems perfunctory at best.

What's your address?

I send it to her without stopping to wonder why. She probably needs it for forms or something. I'm too busy to give it much thought—deep in an emergency advisory meeting to try to clean up the deal that went south with my grandma a few days ago.

So it's not until several hours later, finally done with the world's longest workday, that I read her responses.

Great, I'll be over around 8pm with my stuff.

By the way, taxis from Sunnyside are $$$ at rush hour, so I texted Norm to come help me, hope that's okay.

PS Norm says hi.

When did she even get Norm's phone number?

Moreover, what does she mean "with my stuff"? I check the time on my phone. It's already eight thirty. I groan. If she did randomly show up at my place, she's probably been keeping the doorman company for the last half an hour.

Norm's obviously indisposed, so shaking my head, I descend into the subway—no use even bothering with a cab at this hour on a workday—typing one-handed while I do.

On my way there. What do you mean "stuff?"

She doesn't reply.

It takes me twenty minutes to get to the Upper West Side, where I live in the most desirable glass high rise in Manhattan, right around the corner from the Natural History Museum, with a commanding view of Central Park.

The second I laid eyes on the apartment, I knew I needed it. Never mind the view all the way to freaking Iceland. Never mind the glass staircase to the second floor or the windows that go on for days.

You can't put a price on prestige like this.

I nod to my doorman, Edward.

"Good evening, sir." He tips his hat. "Subway today then?"

I'm about to ask him if Norm's been toting around a young woman in a wedding gown and white sneakers, but Edward rushes off to open a cab door for another resident.

I get out of the elevator that connects to the first floor of my place. No sign of anybody loitering in the hall. Maybe Phoebe gave up her visit? Or maybe she stopped by to drop something off and she's gone already? As I let myself into my apartment, I decide I'll have to call down to Ed.

"Hi, hubby," calls a familiar feminine voice the moment I enter the foyer.

"Um... Phoebe?" I blink, then collect myself and shut the door, climbing a couple of stairs. I look over the banister, thinking maybe she's down here.

Normally everything's kept army sergeant neat by Maureen, my housekeeper, who must have taken a long walk to China or something, because stuff is scattered all across the living room sofas and lounge chairs. Books, notebooks, some towels laid out over the couch, and heaps of T-shirts. I stare at the whirlwind, and my gaze lands on three suitcases, each big enough to hold a person, opened in the middle of the hand-knotted wool rug. She has a damn bedroom for this stuff. At her own damn apartment.

I'm still staring when Phoebe appears at the top of the stairs.

"I assume that big top floor penthouse room with the en suite is yours," she says as she descends. "*Nice* jacuzzi tub by the way. So I claimed that room with the park-facing windows and the walk-in rain shower. Hope that's cool."

"By *claim*, you mean..." I tear my gaze from the suitcases to frown at her in confusion.

She plants one hand on her hip, staring as though *I'm* the one being confusing right now. "As in, to sleep in? Unless you want me to actually move into your room, but I thought that would be weird with the no-sex, not-a-prostitute stipulation and all. Besides, even some real married couples maintain separate bedrooms like in *I Love Lucy*. We can just tell whoever you need to fool with this charade that you snore or something."

Right. We're married now. A marriage that needs to seem real enough to fool my grandmother, one of the world's most legendary self-made businesswomen.

I should have seen this coming. But somehow, for a guy who can see problems in a business deal ten miles away, when I signed the marriage contract this morning, I hadn't quite imagined the part about living arrangements.

I squint as a furry black face peeks out from between Phoebe's legs, green eyes narrowing at me in displeasure. "Is that a *cat*?"

"It sure is!" She picks up the furball and points his face at me. "Roger, meet Easton. Easton, Roger."

Roger doesn't hiss or growl, but I'm pretty sure from the way his eyes narrow in my direction that he does not like me.

I run a hand through my hair. "How did you even get in?"

She blinks in surprise. "Norm talked to Ed, who was totally okay with it, then Maureen let me into the apartment. Norm called her for the keys—she is *such* a sweetheart. Also spoke highly of you, by the by, which is good to know, because you can tell a lot about someone by how they treat their employees."

Betrayed by the kindness of my own people. This is how kings fall. Then again, I can't really blame them. I didn't let Norm in on the whole "this marriage is fake" secret. He knows my grandmother too well for that, and I'm not entirely sure he'd approve, being a big family man himself. And Maureen, well, same.

Phoebe would've needed to move in eventually. I just didn't expect it would be *tonight*.

The cat wiggles out of Phoebe's arms and runs past me, brushing against my ankles. Phoebe follows, but without the brushing part. Which is too bad, because she smells like cookies and sex.

"Gotta admit," she says from below me, gesturing to the huge space. "This isn't where I pictured you living. I assumed you'd be in some Park Avenue prewar with fuddy-duddy furniture. But with a little work, this could be kind of actually... *hip*."

My head feels a little light. There's a buzzing sound in my ears as I realize, for the first time since I proposed this plan to Phoebe, exactly what I've gotten myself into.

I'm no longer in control here.

CHAPTER 6

PHOEBE

I'm able to pack up my entire life, with Monty's help, in a shocking amount of time. A shockingly small amount of time.

The contents of the kitchen came with the place, since three of my roommates were already living here when I rented my tiny closet of a bedroom off the living room. My bedroom is behind a partition I suspect the landlord or one of the other roomies erected illegally, since it doesn't even touch the ceiling, so it barely qualifies as an actual "wall."

Ditto the living room and most of the bathroom stuff, except for the towel set my mom sent me as an apartment warming gift.

Everything else I own still fits into the three suitcases I packed when I first moved into this place two years ago.

"How depressing is that?" I ask Monty, who's perched on my windowsill for a vape break.

Disgusting habit, I keep telling him. But at least it won't piss off my roommates anymore.

"Hey, now you'll have plenty of space—not to mention the budget—to expand your wardrobe," he points out, jutting his chin toward the one suitcase entirely filled with T-shirts.

He's been mocking me mercilessly ever since he got a look at my closet. It's probably a good thing that he's never seen me in anything but work uniforms up until now. Well, that and his mother's wedding dress.

"What's wrong with the basics?" I protest. "They all go together, no mixing or matching required…"

"Sure, for every day. But what about when your new husband takes you out to eat at some fancy Michelin-starred restaurant? You can't wear jeans and a T-shirt."

"Isn't that the point of being rich?" I fire back. "You can wear whatever you want these days. Thank you for one useful thing, Silicon Valley."

"Ugh." He rolls his eyes. "This is New York. Our wealthy elite are a whole different beast."

I cross my arms and narrow my eyes. "I *know*. I've spent my entire adult life waiting their tables, same as you."

"But you clearly haven't considered what it'll be like to *be* one of them," Monty replies.

He turns off his vape and slides the window shut, then bends to help me finish packing the one suitcase entirely filled with Roger's supplies. We've already cornered poor Roger into his carrier. We had to do that first, or the clever little jerk would've seen my suitcases and taken off to hide on the top shelf of my roommate's closet. He somehow always knows when something is up, like a trip to the vet or a move.

"You're the one who told me I should do this," I huff. "You even loaned me your mom's *wedding dress* you were so on board."

"And I stand by my terrible advice. But that wedding was only step one. You need to spend the next year fooling everyone into thinking you and Easton are a real item. That means you'll need to fit in. Make friends with his high-powered, socialite, famous friends. Wear stuff that people in that social stratosphere wear—"

"This ring doesn't count?" I wiggle it in his face. With the matching wedding band I insisted on, it's worth enough to put a person through school. Namely, me.

"It's a start. But you'll need to act like the wife of the richest bachelor in New York. You know, a horrible, laborious job that ninety-nine percent of women and gay men in this city would murder you for a chance at." He smirks.

"The richest husband in New York," I correct. "He's not a bachelor anymore." *And the women of New York will do well to remember that.* Wait, eww. Why do I care? I do not. I fling up my hands. "But fine. You're hired as my bougie life coach."

"If that means tagging along on spa days and shopping binges, done."

My phone dings. I grin, eying the text from Norm,

whose number I made sure to get after my whirlwind wedding this morning. Driver privileges most surely come with the wife position, right? Plus, it beats paying cab fare and wrestling these bags all by myself.

Good evening, Mrs. Taylor. As per our earlier call, I'll be arriving in 10 minutes to pick you up. Let me know if you require any help with your luggage.

A smile blooms across my face. "Yeah, okay. Maybe I can get used to the whole *being rich* thing."

Watching Easton look from my belongings to me and back, then squint at Roger, it occurs to me that maybe he's one of those people who's afraid of black cats. Such a ridiculous superstition. I bend down to scratch Roger's head, but my cat never takes his narrowed gaze off Easton.

"It's okay," I coo, though whether to my husband or my cat, I'm not entirely sure. "You're not allergic, right?" I ask, eyeing Easton.

"No, but—"

"Good. Cause otherwise I'd have to insist that you buy me and your stepson our own penthouse, and *that* would probably look suspicious to..." I pause. "Who exactly are you trying to fool with this whole marriage thing anyway?"

He stares incredulously at me. "It's only just now occurring to you to ask?"

"It occurred to me before." I shrug. "It's just that I

didn't care. But now that I'm all in, I should probably know what style of charade you're going for. Cause I'm warning you right now, if it's a jealous ex situation, I *hate* belittling other women—"

"No jealous exes." He actually laughs. "It's, well…" He steps closer to me, then freezes as Roger hisses. "Dear God. Does it always sound like that?"

"He's not an *it*, he's a *he*. And he's hissing because he doesn't know you and he's suspicious of new people. Here, bend down."

Easton does what I tell him for once, and he holds out a hand for Roger to sniff. I hold my breath, watching. I wasn't kidding about the penthouse. I'll leave right now if there's an issue between Easton and Roger—Easton may be my husband, but Roger is my baby. He comes first.

Thankfully, after a few seconds of suspicious sniffing, Roger peels away from my side to headbutt Easton's leg. Easton's eyes go wide. But after a few seconds of watching the cat suspiciously, his shoulders relax a fraction.

I have to suppress a laugh. "He's not going to bite. I mean, not unless he's really hyper and you start playing with him—pro tip, do not wave your hand around underneath a sheet. He *will* claw right through it. But other than that, Roger's a big sweetheart. And he's usually not a talker, so he's easy to hide from the landlord, in case you've got a no-pet lease."

I do a double-take, reconsidering the gorgeous apartment. I can't believe places like this exist. I mean, sure, I knew they existed. I've seen homes like this on reality shows about housewives or real estate moguls, but I never thought I'd step foot inside one. Much less live in one, even temporarily. There's even a freaking terrace. With views. A terrace with views in New York City is a fortune, even if it's attached to a dumpster. And this place is definitely not a dumpster. It's modern. Except not that ugly black-on-black uncomfortable furniture kind of modern. The tasteful, timeless kind.

I'm really glad he has Maureen to housekeep because Roger's black fur is gonna be super noticeable when he sheds and this is way too much square footage for me to bother with. I squint at the open plan kitchen with the six-burner stove and quartz countertops. I also hope Easton's not real particular about cats on counters.

Easton, meanwhile, laughs. "This isn't a rental, Phoebe. I own it."

Now my jaw actually drops. I whip around to stare at him again, trying to mentally calculate the square footage. My place was, what, twelve hundred square feet between the five of us? This is... I can't even do the math. Whole magnitudes more enormous. "The whole thing?"

"Renovated it myself." He crosses his arms. For the first time, I notice an almost proud expression cross his face. "Well, with the help of a very talented local architect and a team of builders, obviously. But—"

"*Okay*, my husband has a closet artistic side." Against my better judgment, I have to admit I'm impressed. And a little bit intrigued. I thought I had Easton Taylor pegged. I thought I'd met a million just like him. Now...

I shake myself internally. *Do not romanticize your fake husband, Phoebe.* This is a precarious enough situation as it is.

I rise to my feet again, faster than I intended. The motion makes Roger bolt, which in turn makes Easton flinch and back up. I burst into laughter, while he narrows his eyes.

"You'll get used to him," I promise. "Now..." I tip my head back to gaze at the ceilings. They've got to be at least fourteen feet. "Is there an in-unit laundry room? How about a grand tour?"

CHAPTER 7

EASTON

Freaky monster cat and uncanny ability to talk her way into whatever she wants aside, I relax again during her grand tour.

For one thing, I think—as I watch her exclaim over the guest bathroom with its big walk-in rain shower and set of fluffy pure white towels—my family will actually like her. My parents, who eloped themselves after a whirlwind romance, won't find it too strange if I do the same. And she's down-to-earth enough to get along with my grandmother, who's still in denial about the wealth she spent a lifetime accumulating so she wouldn't have to skimp on the finer things in life.

But there's something else too. Watching Phoebe react to every tiny detail is reminding *me* how lucky I am.

Not to mention how nice it is I can help this girl. Give

her a chance to start life debt-free, instead of bogged down like so many people these days.

Yeah, it's just pure philanthropism, I tell myself as she skips up to the top floor ahead of me and I try my best not to stare at her ass and the way it jiggles on each step. Fucking hell, I want to tear off those damn jeans. *Pull it together, Easton.*

We reach the top floor, and she smiles. Just smiles.

Unlike most girls I've had over, who gush and simper and only seem to want to talk about how *expensive* the reno must have been, Phoebe seems genuinely impressed by the place. Against her will, I might add.

"Seriously, this was *your* idea?" she asks, not for the first time, once I point out the raw teak ceiling arches crisscrossing to support a frosted glass skylight.

"My idea was more complicated," I admit, "but not physically possible."

"Like, how?" She seems to really want to know, so I'll really tell her.

I point out the beam from the other side of the bedroom wall and lead her around, trying to casually play off the presence of the bed I'd like to tie her to. "My architect wanted to kill me, but I wanted a vaulted ceiling in here. We settled for more of a bandshell."

When I tear my gaze from the ceiling once more, Phoebe is eying me, her head tipped down, her expression unreadable for once. It throws me off. I'm used to seeing her opinions written all over her face. Right now though, I have no idea what's going through her head.

"Didn't take you for the artistic type," she finally says, whirling away from me to stride across my bedroom to the big panel of windows butted up against a balcony that overlooks the western side of Central Park.

"Because you know me so well after, what, three days?"

She glances over her shoulder, grinning. Just the sight of that grin makes my mind go to forbidden places. "Touché."

Without warning, she spins away from the glass and drops onto my bed, bouncing a little to test the weight.

Christ.

Watching her wriggle with satisfaction, then flop backward onto the mattress, her arms spread out to either side of her, is too much. All I can think about is the under-bed restraint system I installed last summer. How, with one duck beneath the four-poster, I could draw out those straps and have her hands pinned in that position, her legs spread wide next.

Then I'd cut off her T-shirt and blindfold her with it. Peel the rest of her clothing off one garment at a time, making sure to taste every inch of her along the way. I'd run my teeth down the edge of that curved neck, trace my tongue in the hollow of her collarbone. Drag my lips down until I reach that sexy white lace bra I glimpsed earlier, unclasp it, and let her breasts fall free so I could trace her nipples with the tip of my tongue, palm her other breast in my free hand, use my other hand to edge her jeans down those generous hips…

"Easton?" She snaps her fingers in the air between us.

I blink, shaking myself out of the trance I'd fallen into. *Fuck.* Maybe this whole fake marriage thing *won't* be as easy as I thought.

"I said, can I use the washer and dryer? I've got a whole suitcase full of dirty clothes, but I wasn't sure if you were planning on doing laundry."

I wave dismissively. "Maureen comes every day. She'll do any laundry you leave out."

Phoebe rolls her eyes. "I am *not* asking some innocent bystander to sort through my panties."

"Why, are they too dirty?"

What the hell did I just say? My self-control's gone to the dogs.

She fires me a simpering fake smile. "You wish. No, it's just *weird*, okay?"

I spread my hands. "By all means, do more work than you need to."

She slaps the mattress and stands. I try not to notice the way her shirt hikes up as she does, revealing a plane of taut waistline before she catches the hem and tugs it back into place. "So, you didn't answer earlier. About why you wanted to be married in the first place."

"Right." I cross my arms. Force my head back into business mode. "My grandmother needs to retire."

She blinks as if that's the last answer she was expecting.

I speak faster, before she can interrupt with a machine-gun fire of questions—which I'm starting to realize is Phoebe's MO. "She and my grandfather founded Taylor Corporation together. It's kind of her baby. My father was supposed to be the heir apparent, but he decided to be a cardiologist instead and Mom decided that if she was going to be a doctor's wife, she was doing it between New York and Paris—"

"Smart people," Phoebe interjects.

"*So,* it's fallen to me to take his place. But Grandma Sofia's convinced I'm not ready for the responsibility of leading the board. She's big on family and traditions—"

"And she doesn't trust a party-bro bachelor to take charge of her baby. Got it." She's smirking.

"Party-bro?" I raise an eyebrow.

"Well, you certainly do have tabloid photos partying in a lot of cities." She shrugs. "Not to mention your two besties' notorious reputations, and your—what did *People* say? Commitment-phobia?"

"You try having photographic evidence of every single night out you ever go on splattered across the front pages of magazines, and see how tame your life looks," I grumble.

Phoebe raises her hands in surrender. "Hey, no judgment. Just saying I can see where Grams is coming from."

Grandma Sofia will either love or hate this girl. Knowing my luck, the former, then they'll team up. Maybe Grandma will tap Phoebe to run the company and I'll be left in the cold.

"When do I get to meet the old bird?"

"First of all, the fact that you just said *old bird* tells me you're nowhere near ready. We're going to start the family introductions small. Parents first—"

"Hang on." Phoebe's eyes widen. She gets a gleeful expression on her face. "You said your parents live in Paris. Does that mean…?"

"They'll be here next weekend."

The gleeful expression drops into a pout. I feel a weird mixture of guilt for being the one to wipe the anticipation from her face and a pulse of heat. Because fuck, she looks good when she pouts. Maybe because it accentuates how full her lips are. Or maybe because I know she'd look sexy as fuck with her lips swollen after wrapping them around my cock.

I tell myself I can stop this line of thought any time now, but don't take my own advice.

"Okay," she murmurs. "Note to self, drop a few hints about how much I love Paris in spring while we have dinner." Before I can protest, she brightens again. "What movie are we?"

"What?" Her train of thought seems to jump its tracks a lot.

"If we need to sell this whole whirlwind romance thing, we need to pick a plot. Where did we meet? Why did we rush into this? I don't think we can pull off a *Big Fish* style, 'oh time just stopped when our eyes met' deal. What about Jamie and Aurelia in *Love Actually*? Wait, no, that'll never work. I'm not Portuguese and you're not Colin Firth—"

"Can't we just say we met at a bar?" I interrupt.

"Which bar?" she fires back.

I blurt the first name that comes to mind. "Freddy's? It's in Brooklyn. I've been a few times so it's believable. But not often enough anyone from my office would wonder why they've never seen you before…"

"Well, *I've* never been to Freddy's."

"Who cares? We're lying, remember?"

She tosses her hair. "Fine. What was I wearing? Who approached who? What was your opening line?"

"Do you seriously think my parents are going to quiz me about what you were wearing when we met?"

"They might."

"They won't."

"Well, I hope you're right, because if they *do* ask, I'm going to tell them you were wearing a T-shirt with a big rainbow cat on it and I was instantly smitten."

"I thought we were talking about what *you* were wearing," I deadpan.

"Guys can dress to attract dates too." She tosses her hair, smirking. "When did we meet? What day was it?"

I groan, then glare out my windows while I do some quick mental math. "Two months ago? Any longer and I'd have to explain why nobody's ever seen you. Since Max and Dylan are in on this whole thing, they can pretend to have met you, but anyone else…" My stomach tenses. I'm just now thinking about Sydney.

My little sister, currently enrolled at Columbia, takes no greater pleasure in this world than ferreting out secrets. The kid was the bane of my existence growing up, constantly threatening to rat me out to my parents for stashing booze in my room in high school, or sneaking off to Europe with a fling that one time in college...

Granted, she only threatened as a form of blackmail. She's never actually followed through on tattling. And she's busier than ever now that she's enrolled in an investigative journalism course—talk about an appropriate career move.

But still. I should've thought about her before I let Max talk me into this.

Shit.

Phoebe, meanwhile, is pacing, lost in her own thoughts. "Am I pregnant?"

I start. "Excuse me?"

"Well, why in the hell else would you marry a girl you've known for *two months*? They'll definitely all assume I'm pregnant. Unless you've never had a girlfriend before because everyone you've dated ran when you geeked out about your comic book collection or something." She peers under the bed as if she's searching for evidence of geeky comics.

Sudden panic shoots through me. Because if she looks too hard in this room, she'll find a lot more than comics.

Like the harnesses under the bed. The handcuffs in my nightstand drawer. The entire section of my walk-in closet dedicated to various sex toys. Ropes and blindfolds and vibrators are chief among the collection, though one of my one-night stands did forget a set of nipple clamps when she left...

"Let's just stick to the whirlwind romance story." I

cross the room and catch Phoebe's arm. I draw her upright before she looks around any further and decides she's married someone way too kinky for her delicate sensibilities. I guide her toward the staircase. "We can talk details in the morning."

"Mmmmmkay," she replies, sounding more dubious than I've ever heard her.

"What's that supposed to mean?" We stop beside the steps.

She searches my face, her eyes narrowed. "You just don't seem like the world-windy type to me. But hey, this is your family, not mine."

"It's *whirlwind*, not world... windy... whatever you said." I shake my head.

"See, you would never correct a woman you were *world-windy* in love with like that."

"But it's *whirl*wind."

She shakes her head and waves away the actual right way to say it. "Have you seen *Titanic*? Use that as a barometer. What would Jack say to Rose?"

"All I remember about that movie was the fact that she lets him die in the end. They both *obviously* would have fit on that board—"

"And it would have *sunk*, because it was a piece of plywood, not a boat." Phoebe rolls her eyes. "Just watch it again, okay?"

"Are you giving me a homework assignment?"

"I'm giving you advice. But if you don't want my help, fine. Fair warning, I'm going to make up whatever parts of our story I don't know—and I have a *very* vivid imagination."

Me too, I bite my tongue on the retort. *Right now I'm vividly imagining what I can put in your mouth to make you stop talking...*

CHAPTER 8

PHOEBE

The next few days pass in a luxurious *worldwind*. I spent my entire first day in the apartment unpacking and showering. Easton isn't home much, I'm learning. Early riser, usually at work before I crawl out of bed, and he doesn't get home until I've already eaten dinner.

Which isn't a problem for me. I've got plenty to occupy myself with. Reading for my thesis, taking notes for my thesis, classwork in between it...

Plus, I've been taking at least three showers a day—the pressure on this thing is incredible. Not to mention the various settings of the wall jets that massage your body while you're all soaped up.

And, okay, maybe once or twice I let my mind wander to what it might be like to have two people in here.

Just because it's a really big shower, that's all. Not because when I went to sleep that first night, I couldn't stop picturing the flash of heat I glimpsed in Easton's gaze when I jumped onto his bed. Or the way his eyes lingered on my hips anytime he thought I wasn't looking.

Okay, yes, if I'd actually run into Easton at a bar—though probably not Freddy's, which I Googled and it looks like some hipstery hangout—I would've gone home with him without much convincing. I probably would've even let him make me breakfast the next morning, if he were so inclined.

But since he's now my husband, any sort of hookup is completely off the table. That would take this entire situation from *probably a bad idea but at least one I can justify* straight to *what kind of nightmare have I gotten myself into.*

So I'm in denial about the fact that I've woken up on more than one morning since my arrival with a damp sensation between my thighs and a vague memory of a dream where I'm in Easton's bed, straddling him, his hands wrapped so tight around my thighs they leave bruises while he thrusts up into me with a cock big enough to make me ache.

Ugh. I turn the taps to cold just long enough to snap me out of it.

Tonight is meet the family night. I need my head on straight.

I step out of the shower, wrapping a towel around me—a towel that comes straight off a heated rack, so it's warm, like a towel straight from the dryer, when I wrap it around my torso. How genius is that? It's Nobel prize stuff, at the very least.

Back in my bedroom—is it weird I already think of this guest room as *mine*?—my phone is buzzing. Monty. I answer, putting it on speaker while I rub down my limbs. "What's up?"

"*What's up*? I've been texting you for two days straight! I thought you got serial-killered."

"I told you the move went fine," I protest, because I definitely remember texting Monty that first night. And the morning after, with updates about the house.

After that, well... all of my free time left after studying might have gotten used up, after I realized that what I thought was a huge blank wall in one of the spare rooms on this floor is actually an enormous projector setup, complete with built-in surround-sound. It's like being in a movie theater, but without people, so it's better. No sticky soda on the floor. No listening to strangers chewing. Or worse, sneezing.

For a guy who's never home long enough to watch movies or TV, Easton sure has a full-on entertainment system.

"And your name isn't on the schedule anymore." Monty interrupts my home theatre fantasies, reminding me I'm still on the phone.

"Duh. You think I'm going to keep waitressing when I'm married to one of the club's members?" I raise my left hand and wriggle the ring. It winks in the overhead light. I can't imagine I'll ever get tired of watching that sparkle. "I quit the minute we signed that prenup."

"Are you sure you should be putting all your eggs into this one basket?" For the first time since Monty approved this plan, he's sounding dubious.

I glare at my reflection in the mirror. "You're the one who said I should do this! Not to mention, you told me repeatedly I'd need to, what was it you said again? 'Act like the wife of the richest bachelor in New York'? Pretty sure none of the *Real Housewives* waitress part-time."

Monty sighs. "Okay, fair point. But you could at least keep me updated. What's going on? Uncovered any of your husband's deep dark secrets yet? You better not have gone on your first shopping spree without me."

"*Relax.* No sprees yet. Although maybe I should have." I bite my lower lip and consider my closet. A walk-in that's about the size of the "bedroom" I was living in until last week. "I'm meeting his parents tonight."

"Oh, shit. What are you wearing?"

"Hmm. I was thinking maybe my favorite pants. You know, the hot pink ones with BADASS on the butt." I tug the sweatpants in question out of the rack to examine the rhinestones that form the letters against the velour fabric.

"You cannot wear *sweatpants* to meet the *Taylors*."

I can practically hear a vein popping in Monty's temple all the way from here, and I cackle into the receiver. "It's a *joke*, Monty. I'm just going basic LBD."

He exhales. "Thank God. Pair it with heels though."

"Why? Heels are for attracting a fuckbuddy. I'm married now. Do I really have to suffer foot pain for my celibate husband?"

"Is *that* his deep dark secret?"

I roll my eyes. "Hanging up now."

"Send pics of the final outfit," he shouts before I disconnect.

I let the towel drop and consider myself in the mirror. Hold up the dress. *Fine.* I'll wear heels. But I should really get a bonus for that.

"You look nice." Easton's voice stops me halfway down the steps to the main room.

I'm not used to him being here at this hour. Hell, I'm still not used to him, period. Or to living with a male roommate—which is what he is. My roommate husband. Who—I stop in the middle of the steps, my mind feeling like a computer that just lost internet connection.

Easton's gazing up at me with his usual little half smile. He's also only half dressed. Black slacks on, a suit jacket thrown over a nearby chairback. He's in the process of picking up his white shirt, but right now, he's just... shirtless. In the middle of the living room. Pecs and washboard abs and all.

His living room, my brain reminds me. Not like it's weird or anything.

Besides, who am I kidding? I already know what Easton Taylor looks like shirtless. Anyone with Google does. But it's one thing to stare at grainy photos of my now-husband on my phone at night, and quite another thing to be faced with him changing in the middle of the penthouse we now share.

"Uh, thanks. You look..." *Hot as fuck.* "Not ready."

He laughs and shrugs his arms into the shirt sleeves. "Went for a quick run first. Figured I'd need a clear head for this."

He buttons up the shirt, and I can't help it. I stare at those abs for as long as humanly possible, before they disappear behind the starched white button-down.

Who wears a *suit* to a casual family dinner at your parents' second home?

Then again, whose parents have a *second* home to begin with? Mine live in a modest little upstate NY house that could fit inside Easton's living room. When I take the train home to visit, I wear sweatpants and pack a suitcase full of laundry so I can avoid the laundromat on my corner.

Anyway, my brain is still processing the thought of Easton coming home sweaty from a run around Central Park. Maybe I should do my homework in the living room instead of splayed out across my bed...

"You remember our basics?" Easton asks. "Should I make you some flash cards?"

I tilt my head at him, surprised. "How do you know I love flash cards?"

Most of my friends use online study tools, but I'm old-fashioned. I swear I remember things better when it's on a physical piece of paper I can touch.

In answer, Easton juts a thumb toward the kitchen counter.

I flush, realizing I left a spill of flash cards there last night when I wandered down in the middle of a study session to make tea. "I was looking for those!"

Easton rolls his eyes and grabs his suit jacket, starting for the front door. "I imagine you've been looking for a number of your possessions lately, since they seem to be cropping up everywhere. Come on, Norm's already outside."

"Hey, your fault you didn't ask about my messiness before we tied the knot." I jog after him. "Maybe we should claim that was our first fight. You know, make this love story believable."

"My parents don't want to hear about us *fighting,*" he complains. "We're still in the honeymoon phase, remember?"

He opens the door for me when we reach the car, waving Norm back to his driver's seat. As I climb in, I can't help but notice Easton's gaze dropping to my legs. And okay, maybe I take a little longer than necessary shimmying across the back seat, so he gets a better view.

Once we're both shut into the car, Easton reaches across the seat, hand extended to me, palm up. I stare at him for a full minute before I realize he wants me to take it. I lace my fingers through his. They're warm, and they feel strong as they curl around my palm. Protective almost.

There's a flutter in my stomach that I work hard to suppress. *Ridiculous.* But I swear, for a split second when I peer over at my husband, his cheeks are tinted with faint hints of red.

Then he turns to face the window, keeping his hand in mine. "You remember everything I told you?"

"Sydney's the nosy one, yes, I remember. Your dad's a hopeless romantic, and your mom is the one who spoiled you rotten."

"Not sure I would phrase it like that, but..." Still, I catch him suppressing a grin.

We keep our hands locked the whole drive, which isn't a long one. His parents live deeper into the child-rearing section of the Upper West Side. In one of those big brownstones that characters in TV shows are always moving into, even though they'd have to sell an organ on the black market to realistically afford one.

As we're heading inside, Norm taps me on the shoulder. "Good luck," he whispers.

That doesn't exactly inspire confidence.

Mrs. Taylor meets us at the door. "Easton honey! We're so happy you made it." She pulls him into a bone-crushing hug, which gives Easton an excuse to let go of my hand.

My skin still feels white-hot where it was touching his. I shiver and tell myself it's just the night air.

"And you must be Phoebe," Mrs. Taylor gushes. "Come in, come in! We've heard so much about you."

Like what? But I bite my tongue, knowing that's just a thing parents are supposed to say, even if they haven't heard word one about the random new bride turning up on their doorstep.

"Thanks for inviting us," I tell her. "I told Easton we

should've brought wine or something, but he insisted it wasn't necessary…"

"Not to worry, we always bring a case home whenever we visit," a new voice chimes in. "Nothing like the French for wine." Mr. Taylor strides over, hand extended like a caricature of a too-friendly business guy. He shakes my hand so hard I swear my elbow dislocates. "But we'll have to dig into the champagne tonight, I believe. Congratulations are in order!"

"You're kidding me, right?" A shadow appears on the staircase. This must be Sydney—her chin and mouth look just like Easton's, although her eyes are wider and her cheekbones wider set. She's wearing a sullen frown, arms crossed over a Columbia hoodie and matching sweatpants.

I love her instantly.

"If *I* brought home some random husband no one had ever heard of, you'd be locking us both in the house until Anthony came over to annul the marriage on the spot." Sydney tromps down the rest of the staircase to scowl at me.

"Syd," Easton warns, but she just turns that scowl on him.

"No, this is ridiculous. How come *he* can do whatever he wants, but if I do something *way less wild*, you freak out? That's some patriarchal bullshit."

"Ugh, preach," I reply before I can think better of it.

Now Easton's glaring at me, whereas Sydney is eying me with a new expression. Wary, maybe slightly less hostile. "Thanks, but I don't need backup to tell off my own family, random stranger." With that, she storms past our group and deeper into the house.

"Sorry about that." Mrs. Taylor smiles wearily. "She's angry because I caught her in the middle of donating our wedding china to Goodwill when we got home the other night."

"It's not like you *use it!*" Sydney shouts from out of sight.

Mrs. Taylor touches my elbow and gently leads me into the dining room. The table is already set with five places. Someone even folded the napkins into heart shapes on the plates clearly meant for me and Easton.

"Speaking of china, that reminds me!" Mrs. Taylor nudges me lightly. "Where are you registered? We haven't sent any gifts yet!"

Easton's father follows us, with Easton bringing up the rear. "And what about my suggestion the other night, Easton? You two didn't have a big wedding celebration, but surely we can still throw a reception."

"Just something small. Say, family and close friends only?" Mrs. Taylor's eyes light up.

Sydney stomps in from the kitchen, eating ice cream out of a tub. "You have, like, two hundred close friends. Not to mention all the cousins on Aunt Betty's side..."

My face heats up. I trade panicked glances with Easton. He didn't mention his parents wanted to throw us a reception. And the idea of getting gifts from all his family and friends for a fake marriage... My stomach churns.

"Oh no, gifts aren't necessary," I say at the same time Easton speaks up.

"We eloped because we *didn't* want to make a big fuss."

"Don't be silly!" Mrs. Taylor tuts as we all take our seats. Mr. Taylor murmurs something to Sydney about the ice cream, which she pointedly ignores. "We have to get you *some*thing. Maybe a nice wine glass set; Easton only has whiskey and beer glasses at home, typical bachelor." She titters.

Think fast, Phoebe. Otherwise I'll wind up with a house full of expensive china that I can't even donate to Goodwill.

I catch Easton's hand again, squeezing tight. "Really, Mrs. Taylor, Easton is all the gift I need. I don't want anything else. I'm, um... a minimalist."

Easton barely contains a snort.

Across the table, Sydney mimes gagging herself with her ice cream spoon.

But Easton's father practically melts. He's beaming at us, then his wife, then back at us. He looks so openly overjoyed that the guilt in my stomach compounds.

Oh, God, they think I'm Easton's soulmate or something, when really...

Mr. Taylor opens his mouth, and I can just *feel* the sappy father of the groom speech coming, so I interject quickly.

"But if you really want to buy presents, you're welcome to spoil your new grandson!" I laugh, thinking of Roger.

Of course, they haven't heard of Roger.

Sydney's head whips toward her father. "I *told you!*"

Mrs. Taylor makes a quick choking sound, like her water just went down the wrong pipe, and she struggles to clear her throat. Meanwhile, Easton steps on my foot, eyes huge when they meet mine. *Oh, fuck.*

"She's not pregnant," he says, at the same time my face turns bright red.

"I meant my cat!" Now the whole table stares. It doesn't help with the whole blushing thing. "Um, *our* cat, that is. Easton's really taken to Roger actually. I keep catching them cuddling, and Easton doting on him, feeding him all his meals..." I turn a wide smile on Easton, eager to deflect this embarrassment in any direction I can. I ruffle Easton's hair, letting my fingertip linger against his cheek.

He has a calm smile plastered on, but his eyes are anything but. They're filled with irritated fire.

Which only eggs me on more. "He said he never knew he was a cat person until he met me. Now he wants to get another one. We're thinking maybe one or two more to start with, see how they get on with Roger. Of course, if we bought the unit below us, we could foster cats from the shelter too, have a whole house full..." My smile widens.

Under the table, Easton steps on my toes lightly. Presses down in warning. "I believe what I said, *darling*, is that I love Roger so much I wish I could clone him. But since I can't, and since he seems to enjoy his life as an only child, being doted upon by *two* loving parents now—"

"I thought you hated cats," Sydney interjects. She narrows her eyes at us.

"Love changes you." Mr. Taylor sighs happily. "Margaret, remember when we first met and I told you I could never leave New York?"

"It's true." Mrs. Taylor catches her husband's eye, grinning. "I told him I wanted to live abroad, and he said he was too much of a homebody. Would you believe he'd never even *visited* Paris before we went for our first anniversary?"

"Actually, Roger is the one who brought us together," I say, brightening. "We were both at Freddy's bar in Brooklyn, and I went over to talk to him because Easton was wearing this adorable cat T-shirt—"

"As a dare," Easton interrupts, smiling through gritted teeth. "Which, of course, I told her when she started gushing about how great I looked in it."

"But then I showed him pictures of Roger, and he said he looked like the most adorable cat in the universe, and it started changing his mind about his anti-cat stance," I pick up.

"So you're saying you eloped because my brother fell in love with your cat." Sydney folds her hands under her chin and fixes me with such an intent gaze, I'm surprised the truth doesn't just blurt right out of my mouth on its own.

This girl will be a great reporter someday. Or a terrifying one. Maybe both.

"Obviously the cat was just a bonus." Easton catches his sister's eye, and some swift unspoken sibling conversation passes between them, conducted entirely in head tilts and lowered eyebrows. Then Easton lays a hand on my shoulder, his fingers brushing my bare skin in a way that sends shivers along my spine. "Now that you've all met Phoebe though, I'm sure it's quite clear..." He turns to meet my gaze.

This is maybe the closest we've ever sat to one another, thanks to his mother's awkward coupley dinner placement. I can feel his breath tickling my cheek as I catch the scent of his cologne—something oaky that goes straight to my head and makes the rest of the dining room fall away.

"I could not possibly have waited one more day to ensure this woman stays a part of my life," he says, gazing at me with a stupid little besotted half-grin.

And it's fake, *I know it's fake*, but for that split second, I can't help the way my body reacts. My heart picks up its pace, and my breath catches in my throat. I feel my lips parting, my pupils dilating. Well, I can't feel them dilate, but they are. For sure.

I should say something, gush about him in return, but all the words that usually pile up on my tongue are gone at once, as though I've completely forgotten how to speak.

"It was a... *worldwindy* romance," Easton says and winks, before he lets his hand drop from my shoulders.

I laugh under my breath, shaking my head a little before I face the table again, my face feeling hotter than ever. God help me, I might be real-life blushing over my fake husband.

When we look up, everyone is watching us. Mr. and Mrs. Taylor have matching wide smiles of joy. Even Sydney doesn't make a snide comment—at least out loud. She just rolls her eyes.

"You two are the cutest," Mrs. Taylor gushes.

I steal another glance at Easton and find him doing the same to me, our smiles more conspiratorial than anything. But I gotta say... I don't disagree.

CHAPTER 9

The week after dinner with my parents, I have my first dream about Phoebe.

Or at least, the first one I can vividly remember. I've woken up sweating most nights with a vague sensation of bodies pressed together, the scent of vanilla in the air, but this is the first time I dreamt something coherent. The two of us naked in the kitchen. I picked her up and spread her across the counter, poured chocolate across her taut stomach, pooled whipped cream around her nipples, and set a strawberry in the crook of her neck. Then I proceeded to eat it off her, slow and teasing, until she was begging me to fuck her in a smoky voice husky with need.

Only when she was pleading, borderline desperate, did I finally spread her legs and press my tongue between the folds of her pussy. She was soaking wet, and with every lap of my tongue, her body trembled faster, her breathing coming harder, those gorgeous breasts of hers quivering as I ran my thumb across her hardened nipple.

And all the while, she kept saying my name. "Easton, Easton…"

"*Easton*." The sharp voice in my doorway sounds nothing like the one in my head.

I sit bolt upright—which is useful, because the sheets puddle around my waist and serve to hide my raging morning wood.

Phoebe's leaning against my doorjamb wearing yoga pants and a ratty T-shirt, hip cocked so those curves are on full, lush display. Fucking hell. Is she trying to kill me?

"Yes?" My voice comes out gruff. Normal sounding. I hope.

"Can I borrow Norm? I want to take a spin class."

"Sure, okay." I squint blearily at my alarm clock. Sunday.

Oh, shit. Sunday. I'm supposed to meet the guys for a run through the park in… half an hour. I'm about to throw back the covers when I remember my throbbing hard dick, and stop myself.

"Was that all?" I ask the woman in my doorway. A woman who, in my head two minutes ago, I was making scream so loud it echoed through this entire house.

"Roger sprayed on the hallway carpet," she says. "I'd clean it, but I'm running late. Can you rub some stain stick on it and I'll clean it when I get back?"

Well. That solves the hard-on, at least. I rub my

temple. "I thought cats were supposed to be smart. Litter-trained, all that."

"He's just marking his territory. He's protective of his mommy, isn't that right, Roger?" she coos, as the oily beast winds through her legs.

I scowl at him. The cat glares right back. I swear he knows he's pissing me off. Doing this on purpose.

"Fine," I grumble.

"Thanks!" Phoebe jogs downstairs, leaving me alone with the cat.

At least we have one thing in common—we both turn to watch her go.

By my third loop around the reservoir with Max and Dylan, I've finally shaken the remnants of that sex dream. Sweat works wonders for this sort of thing. That, and cleaning up cat piss.

We're on our cooldown, walking out of Central Park at 81st and across CPW toward our usual smoothie cart —listening to Dylan rant about his parents the whole way—when Max pauses. "Hey, isn't that your wife?" He points through a huge plate glass window on the corner.

Sure enough, through the windows, we can see a spin class in progress. A dozen women, all in tight leggings and sports bras, rise in unison on their stationary bikes, peddling as though their lives depend on it. And right in the center—sporting objectively the best ass in the entire lineup, even if I weren't biased, which I'm obviously not because this is fake, is indeed my wife.

In the mirror in front of the room, I can see Phoebe's got on what I've come to recognize as her *game face*. Her brow is furrowed, her jaw set, and her fists balled on the handlebars. God forbid anyone tries to argue with her in that state. In this case, I guess that would be the bicycle?

"Dude, that instructor is *totally* checking out her ass," Dylan says.

For the first time, I notice the class instructor—the only guy in the room. He's moved off of his own bike to yell something that makes all the women lean forward over their handlebars and pedal faster. But I can see his gaze very obviously linger on Phoebe's backside.

Sudden, unexpected heat sears through me.

"Do you think he sees the wedding ring?" Max crosses his arms. He's baiting me like I'm the stupidest fish in the sea.

Dylan snorts. "Pretty impossible to miss a rock that big."

Two hooks down and yes, I'm as dumb as a rockfish.

"Shut up," I snap, though I'm not angry at them. Who *am* I angry at? My marriage is fake, so I shouldn't care about the gym instructor's blatant disrespect. And she's not doing anything, so I can't be mad at her.

Myself.

I'm mad at myself.

With my electrolytes depleted and that dream still running through my head, every nerve ending in my body screams at me to storm in there and tell the instructor to fuck off, when the fact that I never mentioned exclusivity with my wife is one hundred percent my fault.

Max and Dylan trade pointed looks behind my back. Doesn't matter. I can see them in the glass's reflection.

"What?" I demand.

"Nothing." They both raise their hands in unison, wearing twin innocent expressions.

"I need to speak to my wife," I say. "I'll see you later."

They head off, although not before I catch the words *totally fucking.* I scowl at my friends' backs. I've already lost count of how many times I've had to explain to the two of them that my wife and I are not *fucking.*

Maybe that's the problem, whispers a part of my brain I'd rather ignore. *Maybe you just need to fuck her once, get her out of your system. Maybe then you'll stop dreaming about her...*

I manage to shut the voice up, just barely, in time for Phoebe's class to let out. She takes forever in the changing room, which only makes me antsier. I pace the sidewalk until she finally emerges, ponytail damp from the gym shower.

I'd like to get behind her and pull it as I—

She stops short when she sees me, and her eyes light up for a second. Until she notices my expression. "What's wrong?"

I run a hand through my hair. Take a deep breath and shut my eyes to cool down. But when I close them, all I see is the instructor checking her out. "We did make it clear that this relationship is exclusive, right?"

When I open my eyes again, Phoebe's jaw has dropped. She glances over her shoulder at the emptied gym, then hooks her arm through mine and drags me toward the corner, lowering her voice as we go. "You mean this *fake* relationship?"

"We can't fuck other people. Word would get out. It would blow our entire story."

She makes a sound in the back of her throat and shakes free from my grip. "So you expect me to stay celibate for *a year*?"

"Well, there is another option."

For a moment, she stares as though she doesn't understand. I stare right back, deadpan. I see the moment she figures it out, the gears connecting. Her eyes widen, and for one split second, I can see her consider it. And... is that a *blush*?

But then, "We already established that I do not get paid for sex."

"And I agreed. So it's free of charge."

"So I'm a prostitute who gives it out for free?"

This was supposed to be a mutually beneficial addendum to the agreement. How did I get cornered into insulting her? "Pay me, if it's so important to you."

"Dream on."

Dream. Does she know?

Of course not. That's ridiculous. How could she know? She's not psychic. But there's something a little too piercing in my wife's gaze right now. As if she can see right through my irritation to the real problem.

Maybe she can. She'd have a point. What am I even

getting jealous over? Some gym instructor looking at her?

I wave. "Forget it. Just... do *not* fuck a goddamn spin instructor, for Christ's sake. I get enough flack in the tabloids as it is."

Her jaw drops and her eyes widen, but before she can start in on me about the haze of irritation gathering around my head, I walk up the street. If my wife were my usual type, we'd both enjoy her teasing or acting out like this, because I could punish her for it.

But Phoebe Jones is no sub. Which might be exactly why she's driving me so crazy.

CHAPTER 10

PHOEBE

"Monty." I'm sprawled across the couch in the entertainment room, *Pretty in Pink* on pause behind me. Normally it's one of my favorite movies, a comfort watch. But right now, I can't focus.

All I can think about is Easton. The heat in his eyes when he cornered me after the gym. *We did make it clear that this relationship is exclusive, right?* It was almost like he was jealous. Easton Taylor—sharp-eyed, chiseled-jaw, gloriously sweat-stained after his Sunday run through the park, Easton Taylor—stalking me outside of my spin class. Getting jealous over *me*.

In the back of my mind, his words play on repeat, over and over, the way they have been all day.

There is another option.

So of course, I locked myself in here to call my best friend.

"Tell me not to fuck my husband," I say.

I have to shout, because Monty's on break at the Murray Loft. In the background, I hear the usual shouts and bustle of the kitchen, where he'll be eating his shift meal in the corner with Missy and Ray and some of the other employees.

For a split second, I almost miss it. *Almost.*

On my lap, Roger opens one eye, irritated by the noise.

"You mean you *haven't* fucked him yet?" Monty replies, equally loud.

At that, Roger huffs and storms off to the far side of the couch, glaring at me with the disdain only a cat can.

I groan and roll over onto my stomach. I've got a neck kink due to being trapped under Roger for the better part of an hour. He's too cute to move when he's in snuggle mode. "Of course not. That would be a terrible idea. We're *married*, remember?"

"Yes, because having sex with your husband is deeply unusual."

"You know what I mean." On screen, a frozen Molly Ringwald stares at me in silent agreement. "This is complicated enough as it is. Hell, there's a *contract* involved."

"I thought you left the no sex clause unmentioned," he fires back, and I regret how much I share with my best friend sometimes.

"Well, yeah, but—"

"So you *could* fuck your husband. It's not like the fake marriage police are going to bust in and arrest you for it."

"It's a business arrangement. What happens if… I don't know, we bang, and one of us catches feelings, and then we're stuck in this condo together for the next year, stewing?"

"I thought you said it was a *really* big condo…" He makes it sound like he's talking about more than a living space.

I snort. "Not helping. You're supposed to tell me I'm only thirsting because I haven't gotten any in a while or something. That if I avoid him, it'll go away."

"Oh no. What's the old adage?" Monty pauses to chew some food. Sounds like salad, from the crunch.

I pull the phone away from my ear and grimace. I *hate* chewing sounds. But Monty knows that.

When he clears his throat, I listen in again. "Absence makes the heart grow fonder. And that other one. Familiarity breeds contempt."

"So I should spend *more* time with my husband to get over him?" I arch an eyebrow at Molly. Doesn't sound accurate.

"Specifically, spend time with him while he's doing stuff that'll get on your nerves," Monty suggests.

"Like chewing really loudly?" I reply.

He takes an extra-long bite just to annoy me. "Exactly!" he adds once he's swallowed.

"Hmm." Monty does have a point. Not about the chewing—gross. But maybe I *can* stage some quality time with my husband that's guaranteed to turn me off.

Actually… I sit up, brightening. "You're a genius."

"I know," Monty says. "Why, again?"

"I'll report back tomorrow night and let you know."

With that, I hang up and lever myself off the couch. I need to get a good night's sleep if I'm going to do this.

Monday morning, at the ungodly hour of ten o'clock, I step out of Norm's car onto the sidewalk in front of Taylor Corporation. "Thanks again." I lean in and try to pass Norm a tip, but he waves me off.

"I'm salaried," he says, the same way he always does. "Save that for someone who isn't."

I suppress a smile and make a mental note to badger my husband into an extra big Christmas bonus for his driver. And the housekeeper too. Poor Maureen has really had her hands full keeping Easton's white furniture white with Roger shedding black fur like grenades all over.

Seriously though, who buys *white* furniture?

The front doors of the Taylor Corporation are spinning glass. I check myself in the reflection. My clothes are new—courtesy of my first ever shopping trip with actual money in my pocket. I spent an hour wandering up and down Fifth Avenue, enjoying the double-takes all the employees did when they spotted my ring, before I found the perfect outfit. Tight suit skirt, matching little cropped suit jacket, and a silky white blouse underneath —just loose enough to show off a hint of cleavage without being *too* much.

Aside from the hostess uniforms I had to wear in fine

dining, I've never worn anything this formal. Usually I'd rather die than be caught dead in anything business-y, especially in this setting. But eying myself now, I *do* feel a little bit like Meryl Streep in the *Devil Wears Prada*. Much as I hate myself for it, I feel a slight thrill at the thought.

With one last confident grin, I stride into the high-ceilinged lobby of the Taylor Corporation. My heels echo on the marble floor—*click, click, click.* So satisfying.

I make it halfway to the elevators before a security guard chases me down. "Excuse me, miss, we need to register any visitors over at the desk."

I resist the urge to self-consciously check my skirt again. Can he can tell I don't fit in somehow? Is it written on my face, or my clothes, or?

But I follow him to the desk and see the giant row of screens positioned almost but not quite out of sight. Everyone else walking in has a big badge pinned to the lapel of their suit or jacket. Whoops.

Also. Kind of creepy? All the cameras?

Great. This plan will work perfectly. I'll see Easton in his native environment—a.k.a., buttoned-up-boring-as-hell-suit man. That will kill all the gross thoughts I've been having. Thoughts like him tossing me onto that big, firm bed of his, and me enjoying it.

"I'm here to see Mr. Easton Taylor," I say. The guard's eyebrows rise. Just to make them rise higher, I wiggle the ring. "Tell him it's Phoebe. The old ball and chain."

The guard's got a decent poker face. Aside from the eyebrows, he's got no other tell. "One moment." He presses a button, leans one elbow on the desk.

While he's doing that, I scan the wall behind him. The names of the founders are emblazoned beneath the Taylor Corporation logo. *Josef and Sofia Taylor.* There's a photo of them when they must have been around Easton's age now. I stare at it, wide-eyed.

He looks *so* much like his grandfather. Except the hair. He's got Sofia's hair.

The guard murmurs into the receiver, then pauses. Covers it to look at me. My stomach tenses. I'm about to make some excuse, say this was all a mistake—has Easton even told his coworkers about me? Was this some part of the contract I didn't read?

I'll be honest, I skimmed a lot of the denser clauses. Okay, most of it. Contracts are a real dry read.

But then the guard points at a bank of elevators. "Top floor."

Of course.

I smile extra wide as I thank him, then I board the elevator, sandwiched between a man in a three-piece suit who smells like an entire cologne counter got dumped on his head, and a woman in business slacks and a button-down, carrying a briefcase.

"Top secret?" I ask her with a nod at the briefcase.

She stares back at me, not even a hint of humor in her eyes. "No."

Okay then. I turn to face the panel of buttons, and try to ignore the guy's breath. It smells like onions and... whiskey? I squint at his reflection in the doors, trying to determine if he's actually drunk at ten o'clock on a workday. Hard to say. His eyes are red, but he just glowers at the elevator panel, impatiently shifting his weight side to side.

When we finally reach the top floor, he actually elbows me and the other woman in his haste to get off. I scowl at his backside.

See, this is why I hate suits.

This was a good plan. I'll see Easton as an asshole just like him, and voila. Crisis of libido will be cured.

I follow the woman off the elevator and pause at an empty receptionist's desk located directly across from the elevators. A scattering of pens litters the desk, along with a mug of something or other, but no receptionist in sight. Poor guy probably slipped off for a bathroom break at the exact moment the boss's wife strolled in. I should wait, surely. But a stroll through the office unannounced will be more informative, am I right? I weave through aisles of desks. Everywhere I wander, more suits. Men and women, all of them bustling around or chatting in little clusters with deep frowns and serious faces.

Boring.

Passing the break room, I see the most signs of life. A handful of people chatting and actually smiling—gasp! —as they wait for coffee to brew. But even there, everyone looks tense and hurries away to their cubicles before too long.

Some of them shoot curious glances my way. But if anyone wonders what some woman they've never seen before is doing wandering around in a sexy-as-hell new skirt-suit, nobody asks. Nobody introduces themselves or says hello. It's enough to make me wonder if anyone actually knows one another here.

I near the far side of the office. Instead of cubicles, there are offices here, each one with solid wooden doors and busy-sounding noises on the other side. I beeline straight for the big corner office—surely Easton has the corner.

But when I get there, I see a different Taylor's name emblazoned on the plaque. *Sofia Taylor.* And *her* big wooden door, unlike the rest, is open a crack. Through it, I catch a quick glimpse of gray hair done up in a steel bun, sharp eyes behind cat-eye frames. She's in a meeting, talking to someone in a low murmur. But her gaze shifts and catches me looking.

I whirl away, heart pounding.

Grandma. She's the one we need to fool. But I'm nowhere near ready, not prepared for that battle at all, and if she spots me out here...

I practically jog back across the floor, glancing over my shoulder to check whether I'm being pursued. I'm in the middle of that when I smack into something tall and solid. Some*one* tall and solid, who grabs my shoulders with a familiar, sturdy grip.

"Phoebe?"

I turn to face Easton, and...*fuck.* My stomach drops.

Everyone else I've seen on this floor looks busy, important, unfriendly. Soulless even. But Easton Taylor in his home territory is a sight I was not prepared for.

If I thought the shirt and dress slacks he wore to his

parents' house was fancy, I had no idea. He's in a jet-black suit now, pressed within an inch of its life, his shirt buttoned all the way up to touch the base of his Adam's apple, cinched with a tie in a deep emerald color that brings out tiny gold flecks in his eyes, flecks I've never noticed before.

It's more than the clothing. There's a presence to him, emanating off him.

"What are you doing here?" he asks, releasing me.

I turn my cheek just to tear my gaze from him, just to keep from doing something incredibly stupid, like suggesting we go into one of the empty offices nearby and hash this out over a cleared-off desk. Preferably one he just bent me over.

Everyone else seems to sense the same energy I do. I watch subordinates weave around us or pause in mid-step, entranced by Easton, or me, or just wondering who I am, maybe.

"Can't a wife stop by to bring her husband his favorite lunch?" I ask. I reach into my purse and draw out the bag I made Norm stop for en route. Takeout from a cheap junk food place. Chicken fingers and honey mustard.

I'd planned to make him laugh. Maybe annoy him too, in the process. But now… my stomach does a complicated little flip as he accepts the bag without looking inside, his fingers brushing against mine.

"You didn't have to come all this way," he says, in a voice that suggests something different. Curiosity maybe. Or… hope? "But thank you."

I square my shoulders. "Nonsense. Besides, it was on my way!"

He arches an eyebrow. We're nearly at the southern-most tip of Manhattan, after all. "On your way where?"

"To… Brooklyn! Meeting some friends." I clear my throat and take a step back from him. Fresh air rushes into my lungs, as if I've been holding my breath this whole time without realizing. *Fuck, fuck, fuck.* This is completely backfiring. I cast around for something to make him piss me off already. "Which of these death-traps is yours, by the way? I got lost trying to find you." I thumb toward the wall of offices.

But then… Easton points back toward the elevators. To a row of cubicles in the noisiest, least desirable part of the floor. "Actually, I sit over there. I like to be in the middle of things. Makes me feel more connected to everybody—and makes my employees feel less weird about walking up to ask me for things they might need."

Of course he's some equalist type boss. He couldn't be the stereotypical asshole who makes his secretaries cry. "That's… egalitarian, of you."

He laughs. "I try." Then he takes a step closer. Lowers his voice, just for me. "I could find a spare office though, if you had something else in mind…"

Heat races up my neck, into my cheeks.

We've drawn an actual crowd now. People are lingering by other coworkers' office doors and cubicle chairs, just for the excuse to stare at the two of us. More than a few glance at my left hand, and I curl my fingers, self-conscious of the ring for the first time since I put it on.

"No, I..." *Think of a comeback. Throw him off.*

But I can't. Because what he said is way too close to what I'm thinking. Me, Easton, and a locked door. Both of our fancy suits littering the floor. Him spreading my thighs and trailing those thick, strong fingers up my inner thighs, until he tears off my panties, strokes the wet spot I can already feel forming between my lips...

"I should go," I manage to blurt. My breath trembles when I exhale.

"If that's what you want."

The bastard knows it's not. Easton runs his hand through his hair. It makes his shirt go taut over his stomach and pecs, and his right arm bunches up from the motion. *Fuck me.*

But he's not going to. I cannot let us cross that line.

"Just running late, is all. See you at home, sweetie!"

He reaches out—maybe to hug me, I don't know. I dodge the motion and pat him on the shoulder once, the way you'd pat a friend, an acquaintance. A signal to him and me—this ends here. Then I stride back to the elevator, head held high, and try to pretend like this wasn't an utter failure.

CHAPTER 11

The elevator doors have barely closed behind Phoebe—though not quickly enough for me to miss the sight of her ass in that suit skirt. God*damn,* where did she find that? The outfit hugged her every curve, that shirt just begging to be torn off, the skirt was meant to be hiked up after I bent her over a desk...

Fuck.

Did she come here just to torment me?

Not for the first, or the millionth, time, I wish Phoebe was more of my usual type. If she were, I'd take pleasure in my revenge for this. I'd command her to strip and wait kneeling on my bedroom floor. Then I'd make her finger herself for me, watch how she spreads her pussy, where she places her fingers exactly. I'd wait until she was on the brink before I ordered her to stop. To wait. To not come until I allowed it.

Oh, the release would come eventually, and it would be all the sweeter for it.

But this? There's no release. Only constant torture.

"Easton." The voice of Jake, our assistant operational admin, drags my attention away from the elevator, and back to the curious swarm of coworkers I've attracted. "When did you get married?"

Jake's in his twenties and young enough to be amused by his boss's secret wife. Everyone else is just whispering like a bunch of gossip columnists in the locker room.

By tomorrow, the entire office building will be talking about it: Easton Taylor, bachelor extraordinaire, has settled down at last—but with whom?

Maybe this is a good thing. A blessing in disguise. Maybe it will be a more convincing story for my grandmother, who must have already heard about the family dinner last week from my parents—or if not from them, at the very least from Sydney, who has not stopped creeping on my Instagram page since.

Where's the wifey? along with a series of kissy faces, is the comment my little hellion of a sister leaves on every one of my posts now.

So I stopped posting this week. But I can only avoid the rest of the world finding out about Phoebe for so long.

I force a laugh and wave off my coworkers. "Yes, I'm married. Don't feel bad you weren't invited; nobody was. Small ceremony."

"That's the way to go," my secretary, Anna, speaks up

at once. Lord love the woman—who herself is nearly old enough to be my grandmother. "Charles and I had a big wedding, and it was an absolute *nightmare*. Two years of planning and you want to know how much went wrong on the day?"

"Please, share," I reply, even though we've all heard this story a dozen times already.

I catch a few disappointed expressions as people drift back to their own desks to manage other dramas and problems.

If only I could run away from this as easily.

<hr>

If I linger extra long at the office today, well, can anyone blame me? I've got a reason to be nervous. I have to go home to my frustratingly hot wife.

Just the memory of her in that skirt suit today, her high heels making her already long and toned legs look even longer and more toned; and the skirt hugging every inch of her ass, cupping it the way I wish *I* could cup it in my palms, dig my fingers in for grip while I press my cock into her—it's enough to make a man crazy. I spend half the afternoon zoning out in meetings, dropping the ball on projects.

That's my excuse for staying late. I almost convince myself too.

But then I arrive home—in a cab, because I'd never make Norm miss his family time in the evenings—and Phoebe isn't hiding out on what I've come to think of as *her floor*—the second story landing between her bedroom and the built-in cinema where she spends most of her days—but sprawled across the living room couch on what I've come to think of as *my floor*.

I freeze in the doorway, arrested by the sight of her with her hair in a simple messy ponytail, a ratty T-shirt falling off one shoulder, her legs curled up in tight leggings which only accentuate every inch of her body.

How do I find her even hotter like this? I have time to wonder, before she spots me and leaps off the couch, excitement brightening her eyes.

I hold up a hand to stem whatever she's about to say. "A little warning today would've been nice. The whole office is trading rumors about you now."

At least she has the grace to blush. "I wasn't really thinking that far ahead..." She bites her lower lip, and I swear I *feel* the blood draining from my skull, headed straight for my cock.

I need to focus, so I turn away from her and stride into the kitchen. Water will help. *Cold* water. I pour myself a glass and speak with my back to Phoebe. "We'll have to introduce you to my grandmother soon. She'll have heard about you coming to the office by now, and she'll have my head if you meet any coworkers before her."

"I kind of figured." She flounces over to the kitchen counter to spread something across it. "Which is *why* I spent the rest of my day working on this." She sounds so excited I have to turn and look.

Flash cards. A set of yellow and a set of red. I blink in

confusion, until she holds up one of the red ones. FAVORITE PIZZA.

"Red for me, yellow for you." She turns the card around. On the back it says HAWAIIAN.

I lift an eyebrow. "Seriously?" I'm not sure if I mean about the pizza or the flash cards. Probably both.

"It'll be fun! We'll fill them out and quiz each other." She nudges a stack of yellow cards toward me. The topmost is labeled FAVORITE CAT.

A sneaking suspicion dawns as I reach for it. Sure enough, on the back she's already written Roger Jones-Taylor, First of His Name.

I snort. "Shouldn't I fill out my own?"

"That was just an example to get you started." She plops down on a stool and pulls another card from my stack. "Here's a good one. Favorite New York Pizza?"

"That's a different flash card entirely from Favorite Pizza?" I ask.

"Duh." She rolls her eyes.

I suppress a grin. "Joe's."

"*Really*? I had you pinned for a Grimaldi's guy at least."

"I mean, I won't say no to that either."

She writes. I lean in to read over her shoulder. JOE/GRIMALDI/OTHER? PIZZA HO?

I laugh and shove her gently. "I'm not a pizza ho. Not like I said *Domino's* or something."

That earns me a glare. "Just for that, I'm telling your grandmother you ordered us Domino's one night."

"You wouldn't."

"Watch me." She tosses her head, hair sweeping across that one bare shoulder, and it's all I can do to keep myself from plucking the pen from her hand, tossing it aside, sweeping those flash cards off the table, pinning her against the counter, kissing her until she forgets her own name—

Quit it.

I slip a blank flash card from the red stack and root around in a nearby drawer for my own pen. "Favorite Sexual Position?" I ask her as I'm writing.

"Your grandmother will *not* ask me that." Phoebe pauses. Squints. "Will she?"

I tilt my head. Pin my gaze on hers. "*I'm* asking."

Her lips part ever so slightly. There's a slight intake, a breath where I think she might tell me a real answer—and God help me if she does. If it's something a little... unusual, what would that say about her? About our compatibility?

My throat goes dry. The blood in my veins thunders, more and more of it headed southward the longer I watch her breasts rise and fall under that thin T-shirt—is she even wearing a bra? And the more I notice the flicker in her gaze, the faint shiver, the more I don't want her to answer at all.

With a visible effort, she tears her eyes away to focus on her notecard again. "Missionary," she says dryly, shoulders bunched in a way that tells me she's being sarcastic.

She wants me too.

Or maybe that's my ego talking. Being Easton Taylor

has its risks—namely, that I'm not rejected by women often. Maybe I wouldn't recognize genuine disinterest. Maybe I'm pushing too far.

But when Phoebe peeks at me from beneath her fall of hair, slyly, from the corner of her eye as though she thinks I won't notice... *No.* I'm not imagining this tension. It's real, and it's not going to be ignored away.

Maybe the only way to deal with what we both know is there is to get it out of our systems once and for all.

And besides, what's so wrong about wanting to seduce my wife?

CHAPTER 12

PHOEBE

"Ready for this?" Easton asks, his voice pitched low.

"Depends. How accurate were your Grandma Sofia flash cards?" I murmur.

We're entering Sofia's favorite restaurant, a little Italian spot deep in the Village that I recognize from reading one of those "old school New York" articles. Inside is a narrow, unassuming row of tables, made to look like a trattoria teleported here straight from the streets of Milan. The only nod to the restaurant's history are the pictures on the wall: row after row of celebrities dining here, arms around various members of the staff while they pose.

I have to smile. It reminds me of the first restaurant I ever worked in, up on Restaurant Row by the Theater District. The Broadway stars would stop in—usually for lunch since they'd be performing in the evenings, unless it was a matinee day.

I'm still smiling when an older woman at a table in the back flags us down. "Easton. And Phoebe, I presume?"

I recognize her from all the press photos about Taylor Corporation—not to mention that split second I glimpsed her through her office door. But it's not until she rises to allow Easton to kiss her cheeks that I realize she's almost a full head shorter than me. She looked so tall on camera.

Then again, when she beckons me forward, I feel small anyway. She doesn't offer me her cheek. Just her hand, as though this is a business meeting.

"You're prettier than in the tabloid photos," she tells me as I shake her hand. Her death grip is so tight I barely manage to avoid wincing. She smirks as though she's used to that reaction.

"So are you," I reply, though I'm thinking *holy shit, what tabloid photos?* And, *I hope they weren't of me leaving the gym.*

Monty's advice comes back to me. I'm going to have to get used to this now.

Grandma Sofia has a low, husky laugh. "Don't try to charm an old woman. We've seen all the tricks in the book." She gestures us to our seats.

"Well, maybe so, but I'm obliged to try anyway. Speaking of which..." I dig into my tote-bag-sized purse and withdraw the bottle of scotch it took me an entire weekday to track down last week. Let's just say it's a whiskey that's old enough to legally drink itself and then some. I also obtained a spool of really overpriced ribbon and wrapped a fancy bow around the neck, in what I hoped was an effortlessly chic attempt at rich person gift wrap. "Easton mentioned this was your favorite."

I place the bottle on the table between us, and Sofia's eyebrows rise, just for a second.

I suppress a grin. *Good.* She likes it.

Then Grandma rounds on her grandson. "So you've decided to bribe your way back into my good graces, hmm?"

But Easton is staring at me, clearly surprised. "Phoebe... you didn't have to do that." His voice comes out low, rough with some kind of emotion I can't determine. Maybe he's just feeling guilty about the whole *we're faking it* thing.

I shrug, trying to put him at ease. "Don't worry. I used your credit card."

Sofia cackles. "Atta girl." Easton opens his mouth, but his grandmother cuts him off with a wave. "No, you I'm still angry with. I cannot believe you *eloped*. Did you know I've been saving the cufflinks your grandfather wore at our wedding all these years so you could wear them at yours?"

Easton glances at the scotch. "If you don't want any bribes..."

"I never said that." Sofia snatches up the bottle and tucks it into her own purse, with a quick wink in my direction. "Just that you're going to have to try a lot harder. And don't let your wife do all the work either."

Sofia leans toward me conspiratorially. "If you want to train your spouse correctly, you need to start early. Anytime he drops the ball on chores, or housework, or childrearing—"

"Christ, Grandma, we *just* tied the knot. We're not popping out babies anytime soon," Easton grumbles.

"Just kindly but firmly inform him that he's half of this partnership and you won't pull his weight for him," Sofia continues as if her grandson hadn't spoken.

"That's... really good advice, thanks," I reply, meaning it.

"You don't get to my age—or my job title," she adds, with a long side-eye at Easton, "without learning a few tricks. Now, what's this about no babies yet?" she asks, just as I take a sip of my water.

I choke.

Easton offers me a napkin and scolds his grandmother for trying to scare off his wife—"She can't scare that easily if she married *you*"—until a waiter stops by to take our order.

We make it through appetizers before Sofia starts in again.

"So this really wasn't a shotgun situation?" She gestures between us. "Not that I'd disapprove, mind you. That's why your grandfather and I got married so quickly; I was already pregnant." She nods at Easton.

"Was there an actual shotgun involved?" I can't help asking, completely charmed with Grandma Sofia, as I'm already thinking of her.

"Thankfully it wasn't necessary. But if Josef *had* tried

to run, well, I'm not saying it would've gone well for him… big family, you know. Lots of brothers." Her accent, which has been faint up until now, suddenly bleeds thicker into Eastern European.

Hometown: Pécs, Hungary, I remember from one of Easton's flash cards.

"Grandma likes to imply she grew up in the mob," Easton cuts in.

"I do *not*. If certain people erroneously make this assumption when they meet me?" She shrugs one shoulder. "Not my fault Americans have strange preconceptions. It does make boardroom meetings more entertaining though."

A shadow crosses Easton's expression. I think about the reason he told me he's doing all this—so his grandmother will think he's settled enough to hand over the company reins. But why exactly? Is it just her age? Because he's eager for more responsibility and a higher paying job? Or… is it something else?

I can't help but notice that when Sofia raises her wine glass for a sip, her fingers tremble around the stem, ever so slightly.

For all her tough exterior, she's still getting older.

I search for a topic shift. Something to wipe away Easton's worried frown. "Speaking of boardroom conquests." I rest one elbow on the table and lean my chin in my hand. "Easton tells me you've got some good stories there."

Sofia's eyes light up.

Actually, I believe the exact flash card was: GRAND-

MOTHER'S FAVORITE TOPIC OF CONVERSATION, with Easton's response scribbled on the back. *Corporate War Conquests.*

Across the table, my husband relaxes as Sofia launches into the story of how she talked one of the biggest investors in New York City into taking a chance on her and Josef's fledgling company. When he catches me watching him, he nods ever so slightly in thanks.

That faint hint of approval remains on his face all through dinner, as we listen to saga after saga. Part of me wishes I could politely take notes—Grandma Sofia is fascinating. I could learn a lot from her, even though I don't plan on entering the business world. It never hurts to know how to stand up for yourself and bargain for what you want, especially as a woman.

By the time we've finished dessert—and shared small glasses of the whiskey Sofia insisted on cracking open, despite my protests that I'm more of a vodka club kind of girl—my smiles and questions are all completely genuine. I *like* Sofia. Just like I liked Easton's parents, and even his suspicious, sarcastic little sister.

Which makes this whole dinner sit a little uneasy in my stomach. Because what happens when they find out this was all fake? Except they'll never know that, right? Instead they'll believe I walked out on Easton after only a year of marriage. That must be his plan. We never quite discussed the breakup, but it's not logical that he'd break up with me. I'll have to break up with him. What will his family think of me then? Why does it already matter to me?

What will it feel like to lose Easton after spending a year with him? After learning so much about him? After *living* with him, and actually liking him, as a person? Hell, I'm already starting to feel like I know him on a deeper level than most of the guys I've dated.

Maybe we can stay friends, a little voice in my head suggests. And just as quickly, a louder voice counters, *We aren't friends.*

I've never fantasized about my friends. Friends have never left me waking up coated in sweat, the way I did just this morning, with a hint of a dream lingering in my mind—me on my knees on Easton's big balcony, my lips wrapped around his cock as I made him moan so loudly even my dream self worried it'd be loud enough for the neighbors to hear over New York traffic.

No. Whatever this messy situation is, it's not friendship. But the thought scares me. Because it's not strictly business either…

CHAPTER 13

EASTON

It takes a week after the meeting with my grandmother —a meeting that Phoebe absolutely nailed, going above and beyond what I ever could have expected—before I crack.

Granted, some of that cracking might have to do with the fact that Max and Dylan spent half of said week badgering me about whether or not I was tired of banging the same girl for weeks on end yet. I didn't explain that in order to get tired of a thing, you need to do it a few times. Or even once, which I haven't. Instead, it's been slow, silent torture of a different kind of thing entirely.

Thing One: Walking downstairs, running a bit late to work, I glimpse Phoebe padding across her bedroom in nothing but a towel to shut the door between us.

Thing Two: Coming home to find her sprawled on

my couch in her usual T-shirt, and seeing she's not wearing a bra because of the way her nipples jut through the thin fabric.

Thing the Third: Spending every night before I fall asleep fantasizing about her, and waking up to morning wood so hard it's painful.

I'm convinced I've endured more than any lesser man would've been able to stand.

So, finally, I make up my mind.

The only way to get her out of my head is to fuck my wife.

One problem. I've only ever seduced women I barely know. Preferably ones I meet in casual settings—bars, restaurants, nightclubs, my friends' Hampton yacht parties on holiday weekends, ski resorts in the Alps, that kind of thing. I have no idea how to approach a woman living in my house. One whose favorite color, animal, dessert, and dream vacation idea I already know.

The best place to start is to move said woman to a setting where I'm on more familiar ground.

"Let's go to the bar," I declare that Friday after slipping out of work early. I'm still hanging up my coat, but I'm raring to get this thing going.

Across the main room, Phoebe is tucked in the center of a spray of books. Roger is perched on her lap and glaring in my direction, like he can sense my intention to steal his mother away for the night.

"What bar?" she asks, scribbling something in a notebook. "I'm not hiking all the way to Brooklyn if this is some 'we need to visit Freddy's to make our story more believable' pitch."

I laugh. "No subway necessary. Just the corner pub."

She sets the enormous textbook she's been reading on the coffee table and pets the devil cat, squinting at me with clear suspicion. "Why?"

"Why not?" I counter.

Those big eyes of hers narrow further. But after a beat, she sighs. "Fine. My brain is so fried, I've just been reading the same paragraph over and over for the last fifteen minutes anyway." She flings her body to a standing position, startling a grumpy noise out of Roger. "Let me put on jeans or something."

She's wearing her usual leggings and T-shirt combo.

"You look fine," I tell her. "I mean, great. I mean, it's just a corner bar, so nothing fancy—"

"Did you just call jeans fancy?" She raises an eyebrow in suspicion, then breaks into a smile. "I'm having a good influence on you already, hubby." With that, she jogs upstairs.

I can't help watching her go. It only solidifies my resolve to seduce her. Christ, does she even know what a fantastic ass she has?

You'll need a better opening line for your wife, the voice in the back of my head scolds. It needs to shut up, but it has a point. I can't be lazy about this, but how am I supposed to do it? Where do I start?

Start by drying off your palms, buddy. You're going to dehydrate if they keep sweating like this.

Could I actually be... *nervous*? No way. Impossible.

I've never been nervous about seducing a woman. Then again, I've never tried to seduce a woman who might actually turn me down either. New territory all around.

Phoebe returns in jeans that somehow manage to accentuate her ass even *more*, which should frankly be a crime. One that I'd be happy to cuff her for. Instead, I lead the way up the block to the type of unassuming Irish pub you can find in any decent-sized city in America. Inside, I let Phoebe choose a wooden booth while I order us drinks.

When I join her, I make sure to slide in next to her, rather than across.

She smirks. But if she suspects what I'm doing, she doesn't call it out. She just accepts the drink and gives it a sip before nodding in approval. "You remembered."

"Phoebe's Favorite Cocktail," I recite, a mental image of that particular flash card darting through my mind. "The Cosmopolitan."

She grins. "And my Favorite Alcoholic Beverage in general?"

I shift a little closer on the bench. Let my leg brush hers casually. Am I imagining it, or does she shiver a little at the touch? She doesn't move away. In fact, she presses her leg back into mine, harder.

"Is this a pop quiz?" I ask before taking a sip of my beer.

"Yep. Are you stalling?"

"Nope. Rosé. Specifically, French rosé from the Provence region."

Her grin widens. She takes a long sip of her drink, then leans closer. "Can I confess something?"

Maybe this will be simpler than I thought. I face her. Dip until our faces are only a few inches apart. "Go for it."

Her eyes dart back and forth, searching mine. Her pupils dilate. Because it's dark in here? Or because she's thinking along the same lines I am?

She licks her lips, and I can't help it. I glance at them. Imagine the way she'd taste if I kissed her right now. Like the sweet drink in her hand, mingled with the flavor I caught at our wedding, the first and only time we kissed. Raspberry lip gloss and that hint of vanilla.

The thought is enough to send my blood racing.

"I made up the whole French thing to sound bougie," she whispers. Then she leans away from me, giggling, and picks up her drink for a longer gulp.

"My turn," I say.

"Your turn to be bougie?" She raises an eyebrow.

"My turn to quiz you." I lean on my elbow. Drop my hand so it rests on the bench between us. "What's my favorite position?"

A flush creeps up her neck. She's trying her best to play it off, but I know her by now. I can tell she's about to blush. "Not fair. That doesn't count."

"Why?" I arch a brow. "I wrote a flash card for it."

"I mean... that wasn't... I didn't look at the ones that didn't seem... relevant."

"So it's not relevant to know your husband's favorite sexual position?" It's my turn to smirk.

She glances at me. Away again, fast. Like she's afraid of what will happen if she lets herself linger. "It's not like your family is going to quiz us about our bedroom fantasies."

"Ah." I tilt my head. Lift one hand to catch a stray lock of hair that escaped her ponytail. I tuck it behind her ear, gratified when a visible shiver runs through her shoulders. "So you admit to fantasizing about me."

"That's not what I—" She swallows, raises her drink, and downs the rest in one go. "Fine. Standing up. With *suspension*, whatever that means."

"Handcuffs," I say, and she nearly chokes on the dregs of her cocktail. I grin. "So you *did* read it."

"I skimmed."

"And you remembered." I lean in to close some of the gap between us. Heat radiates off her in waves. "Yet you never filled out your card with the same question."

She opens her mouth. Closes it again. Clears her throat. "I mean. There are only so many positions out there..."

I raise an eyebrow. "Challenge accepted."

"That wasn't a *challenge*." She laughs. "I just mean, like, mathematically. There are only so many ways human bodies can fit together. Guy on top, girl on top, from the front, from the back, horizontal, vertical. That's... whatever six times six is."

"There are more than just thirty-six positions, y'know." I smirk. "And that's not even getting into if you use toys, or swings, or rope..."

"Is it warm in here?" She tugs at the collar of her T-shirt. Her voice gets faster. "It's warm in here, right? I'm going to get a refill. Do you want one?"

I lift my still mostly full beer. "I'm good."

Then I turn sideways, rather than standing, so she has to climb over me to get out of the booth. Her legs brush against mine, and for a second, her ass juts against my chest.

Fuck. I need to make this happen or I'm going to die.

But once Phoebe pays for her drink and returns, she takes care to sit on the opposite side of the booth, avoiding my gaze.

Shit. If I'm misreading her and she's really not into this… I sit there, torn. I could've sworn she felt this too. Not to mention, I'm definitely not imagining her double-takes anytime I come home from jogging in the park, still drenched in sweat. Especially on the warmer days when I run shirtless.

When did marriage get so complicated? I wonder.

But I already know the answer to that. *When I got married to the right woman for the wrong reason.*

CHAPTER 14

PHOEBE

I wake up with a hangover. Probably because I compensated for Easton's sudden flirtatiousness—that was flirting, right, my husband was flirting with me last night?—by drinking far too many cosmos. He was the consummate gentleman, escorting me home and making me a grilled cheese before he sent me to bed with the world's largest glass of water and instructions to drink the whole thing, no cheating.

I woke up to use the bathroom at least three times overnight, but my head isn't throbbing anywhere near as hard as it normally would after a night like that, so it must have done the trick.

Downstairs, I find the house empty, but a flash card with the words EASTON'S FAVORITE HANGOVER CURE is taped to the fridge. I turn it over. Written on the back, in his nearly illegible scrawl, it says *Bodega breakfast burrito. Reheat for 1 min.*

Sure enough, inside the fridge is a burrito from the bodega a few blocks away, waiting on a plate for me. I reheat it and devour the whole thing in enormous bites. He was right. It does hit the spot.

After that, I lie on the couch in the entertainment room and watch *Breakfast at Tiffany's*. But my heart isn't in it, not even when I watch Audrey Hepburn admiring all the jewelry and I hold up my own ring to compare.

What *was* that last night? Does Easton want to add a sex clause to this marriage?

Do *I?*

Because when we were sitting in that booth, pressed so close I could feel his heartbeat through the pulse of his thigh, and it felt like I could drown in his familiar scent, all woodsy smoke and pine from his shampoo and toothpaste, plus a hint of salt and musk underneath that was pure Easton... All I wanted to do was shove him out of that booth and drag him home by the hand to pin him against the door and drop to my knees in front of him.

Plus, his answer to that sexual position card... my stomach tightens.

Standing up. With handcuffs.

I've tried a little light kink before, but it was me using a guy's tie to tie his hands behind his back, rather than the other way around. I thought dominant guys weren't my type—and they aren't generally. They're usually the worst kind of assholes. But Easton... Easton is different. I *know* him. He wouldn't push me into anything I didn't want to do. And I'd be safe.

More than that though, he just has this... way about him. This confidence that tells me he knows what he's doing. That he could show me a thing or two, if I'd just hand over control. And there's something tempting about the idea. Surrendering to my husband. Letting him take the reins.

At the very least, I'm curious.

Which is why, against my better judgment, I find myself at a lingerie store a few hours later, picking out the laciest, silkiest, fanciest-looking pieces of lingerie I've ever seen.

Look, a girl can only stay celibate for so long. And if I can't fuck other people, well...

Like Easton said. *There is another option.*

I make it back home in plenty of time to change into said lingerie before Easton returns from wherever he went this morning. Knowing him, probably the office, even though it's a Saturday.

But when he comes in the front door, he's carrying... shopping bags? I don't pay too much attention. I'm already rising from the couch, letting the blanket I was wearing for warmth drop as I do. Super casually, obviously.

Easton freezes in the entryway. The shopping bags drop from his hands, and he doesn't even seem to register it. He's too busy staring at me. "Phoebe?"

I saunter across the apartment, making sure to take my sweet time about it. Apparently my first-ever fancy lingerie trip must have been a success, because Easton's eyes go to my hips, and don't leave again as I sway toward him. I stop a few paces away to size him up.

"Wh-what are you doing?" There's something gratifying about hearing the faintest stunned stammer come out of Easton Taylor's mouth. Normally he's too poised for that.

Now he knows how I felt last night. Thrown off my game. Surprised. Two can play this game though.

"Helping you with the groceries," I tell him.

Okay, not my finest pickup line. But I've spent weeks living with one of the hottest men I've ever met—and I've been really wound up with all the studying. Not to mention the fact that I haven't gotten laid in... too long. I can hardly be held responsible for the stupid bullshit I say at this point.

Easton runs a hand through his hair. When he moves again, the faint hint of nervousness is gone. A slow smile spreads across his face, a fire in his gaze that wasn't there a second ago. I have just enough time to think, *What am I getting myself into,* before he reaches me, stops right in front of me, and lets his gaze sweep over my body, drinking me in so hard I swear I can *feel* it.

"Phoebe." The subtle command in his voice makes me look up, meet his gaze without even questioning it. "I need to know. Do you want this?"

"I should think that's obvious." I gesture at... well, everything.

"Because we said going into this—*you* said, very clearly—"

"No sex, because I'm not a hooker. Yes. I'm still not." I hold his gaze steadily. "I'm just a woman who wants to fuck her husband."

He arches a single brow, the motion at once thrilling and the tiniest bit intimidating. "Good." Then he closes the gap between us, and before I even realize it's happening, he cups my chin and pulls me into a kiss.

We kissed once before, of course. At our wedding.

This is nothing like that.

His mouth crashes over mine. His lips part mine, and his tongue presses into my mouth, eager, but not overwhelming. He toys with my tongue for a moment, just long enough to make my breath catch and my head spin. Then his mouth is gone again, and he's kissing down the arch of my neck, his teeth every so often brushing over my skin. Not a bite really. Just a reminder that he could.

My hands circle him, press flat against his back. I trail one hand up to cup the back of his neck, let the other sink lower, past the waistband of his jeans, until I reach his ass. I grip it, hard, and I'm rewarded with a throaty laugh, Easton's breath hot against my neck.

"Eager, are we?"

"Mm, you have no idea." I let my head fall back as his tongue circles my clavicle.

His hands fold around my waist, holding me upright. Thank God, because my knees feel weak. Jittery.

Fuck all my concerns. This is a very good idea.

Then one of his hands follows the same path mine did and slides over the curve of my hips until he grips my ass tightly. It's a lot easier for him, since only this skimpy lingerie separates us. I feel the searing heat of his palm, the dig where his fingers press into me. A faint moan escapes my throat before I can stop it.

In response, Easton presses the full length of his body against me, and oh, *fuck*. I can feel his cock, hard as a rock against my belly.

"I've been dying to fuck you since the first day you walked into my house," Easton growls against my neck.

He dips to press his face between my breasts. His other hand traces the bra to the clasp in the back. And maybe Easton is more of a playboy than the magazines and media seem to indicate after all, because he undoes the clasp in less than a second flat, letting my bra spring free and fall down my arms.

He steps away just long enough to toss it aside. While he's doing that, I grab the lapels of his shirt—a button-down for casual weekend shopping? I tear it open and send buttons flying in every direction, baring those gorgeous, rock-solid abs of his.

"Am I supposed to feel bad?" I ask, flicking him a pointed look, before I trace my hands over those pecs. Trail them down to his washboard abs. "You walk around looking like *this* every day, I mean… Fuck."

He smirks. "That's the idea." But he steps back, putting space between us and making my lower lip jut in a pout. Until he meets my gaze again. "Back up." He points at the wall.

My pulse skips. I've never had a guy tell me what to do before. At least not in a way I was willing to respond to. It's kind of… *hot*.

I back the few paces to the wall, aware of Easton's gaze on me the whole way. My nipples are getting hard just from the cool air.

"God, you are fucking perfect," he murmurs, almost to himself.

It's hard to suppress a shiver of desire. My backside bumps against the wall and I stop, breath catching as Easton closes in on me again, bending so his face is inches from mine. My lips part in anticipation. But he doesn't kiss me. He bends to trail his lips along my collarbone. Then down, between my breasts. He catches one breast in his hand, his fingers gently rolling my nipple between them. With his tongue, he draws circles around my other nipple. Then he grazes his teeth over the very tip, drawing another shudder from me.

"I love it when you do that." He looks at me, his gaze hooded. "When you lose control."

His free hand trails along the edge of my lace panties. He pauses at the top of my mound, then keeps going, circling around my hip. Not quite touching me. Not where I long for him to anyway.

"I haven't... lost control," I protest, a little of the breathiness giving me away.

"No?" He arches a brow. "We'll have to see about that." He bends to kiss the plane of my stomach again. Flicks his tongue into my navel. "Spread your legs."

There it is again. A thrill, a pulse shooting through my belly, all the way down into my toes.

I do what he says and inhale sharply at the same time. I can already feel myself getting wet, slick against the lace. The wetness becomes a throbbing, aching *need* when Easton's fingertips trace back over my panties and down to grip me between the legs, gently, just hard enough that I can feel his hand through the panties, cupped against me.

At the same time, he grins, his chin touching my belly. There's something so fucking sexy about gazing down at him on his knees in front of me. "We're getting closer to losing control."

"No, we're... just fine," I manage. My breath hitches again.

He slides both of his hands around to my backside now, cupping my ass tightly enough to pull my hips off the wall and toward his face. He presses his mouth to the fabric, kissing me through it, his tongue pressing against the already damp lace. He teases me, traces his tongue against my mound with my panties still separating us, then draws back.

"I don't know... you seem fairly excited." He kisses my upper thigh. My hip. Lets his teeth graze my skin lightly before he bites the edge of my panties. In one smooth motion, his teeth tug them down my hips until they puddle around my ankles.

I whimper, and Easton's smirk widens. "Case in point."

I bite my lower lip, unable to dispute that one.

I expect him to gloat. Instead, he spreads my legs with his hands and trails his tongue up my inner thigh, all the way to the crease where it meets my hip. Then he arches across my mound to the other side and does the same thing. Teasing. Toying with me.

"Easton…" My voice quivers a little.

"Did you want something, wife?" His tongue dips closer. Closer. He's inches away from my pussy lips, and I know he must be able to tell how turned on I am, how ready to burst.

But I don't want to give him the satisfaction. I shut my eyes, lean my head against the wall. Try not to shiver when his tongue feathers across my clit, so lightly it draws a desperate moan from me. My hips buck up off the wall, and I reach down to bury both hands in Easton's hair, but—

"Ah, ah." He pulls back, sitting on his heels to arch a brow at me. "Hands spread. At your sides."

I'm breathing hard. My pulse is erratic, skipping. "Really?"

He just eyes me patiently. So I swallow my burn of desire and obey again, spreading my hands flat against the wall on either side of me.

"Good." He smiles again. "You'll beg for this."

Before I can reply, he presses his face between my thighs, his tongue pressing right between my lips and into my slit. He laps at me, running the flat of his tongue all the way up to the base of my clit, almost touching it, then sliding back down again. Back and forth, his lips spread against my shaved ones as though he's French kissing my pussy, hungry for me.

Every graze of his tongue sends sparks all the way to my nerve endings. "Fuck, Easton, you… that…"

He smirks, enjoying my breathlessness. "You taste fucking incredible, by the way, Mrs. Taylor."

Then he curls his tongue against my entrance. Pushes until the tip slides inside me. He presses deeper, arches his tongue to drag it along my front inner wall, drawing a faint cry from me. The heat that has been building in me for days—weeks, if I'm honest—cries out for relief. I'm desperate to come. So desperate, I rock my hips against his face, trying to arch up into him.

Easton pulls back again, and I mewl in frustration. He just laughs, the bastard. "Do you want me to make you come, Phoebe?"

I bite my lower lip again, harder this time. Then I nod.

He arches a brow. "Say it out loud."

"*Yes*. Please."

"All of it." His breath ghosts across my pussy, searing hot now that I'm wet from my juices and his tongue. He circles his tongue around my clit. Flattens it and trails it across my clit in one long stroke.

"I want to come, Easton. *Please*. Make me come."

"That's better."

This time, he licks me harder, faster. His tongue slides up my slit, over the nerve-ending spike of my clit, and back again. Again.

I'm so fucking close I can taste it at the back of my throat, feel the tingle in my fingertips, my toes, as I near the edge. But right at the very peak, Easton moves. Stands. I moan in desperation, but before I can say anything, his mouth is on mine. He kisses me hard, deeply. His tongue still tastes like my pussy, and the combination of flavors makes my head swim.

My clit feels swollen, throbbing with want. I'm burning, I *need* this, more than I ever have. We break apart, and his gaze focuses on me, searing hot.

"When I make you come, it'll be with my cock inside you," he says, sending another pulse through my entire body.

I forget about the hands rule, forget about everything but Easton. I grab the clasp of his pants, fumble with it. He takes over, undoing it himself and letting them drop. His boxers follow a second later, and, *fuck.*

"You're so thick," I murmur, before I catch myself. The last habit I need to start is stroking his ego. It's true though. For a moment, the sight of his cock pulls me from the haze, at least long enough to appreciate the length—and even better, the girth.

A vein throbs along one side of his shaft, and there's a pearl of precum gathered at his tip. I catch it on my thumb. Smear it across the head as I grip his shaft in one fist, slowly moving my grip up and down his length. He lets out a low groan in the back of his throat, and I smile.

"Two can play at the torture game, you know," I tell him.

But before I can get him too far, Easton bends to pick something from his pocket. He tears the condom open with his teeth, rolls it onto the length of him, and thank you Jesus that is a nice cock.

Then he raises one of my legs and guides it to hook

around his waist. Positions himself at my entrance. Meets my gaze. "I guess we're consummating this then."

I laugh, but it comes out breathy, barely there. "Might as well."

"Might as," he agrees, but it's more of a grunt.

Then he pushes into me slowly, maddeningly so. An inch at a time, letting me feel every bit of his length. My pussy throbs and tightens of its own volition as I adjust to fit him.

It feels so fucking good. Like he's filling every inch of me, stretching me to my limits.

"You know you've been driving me wild," he murmurs, his mouth at the crook of my neck. He shifts until his teeth graze the sensitive spot just beneath my ear.

The words send a thrill through me. Make my stomach tighten, even as he draws back a little, thrusts into me again, a little harder this time, a little faster.

"I've dreamed about fucking you. Imagined this..." He pulls out again, thrusts back into me once more, hard enough to grind my ass against the wall.

In response, I tighten my leg around his waist. "You're not the only one," I say, my voice so low I think maybe he'll miss it.

But judging by the way his eyes find mine and the heat in them redoubles, I'm sure he heard me. He catches my other thigh and lifts me completely off the floor, keeping me pinned against the wall, so I'm forced to wrap both legs around his waist, which only serves to open me more fully.

"Gotta admit," he says, that hint of a growl still in his voice, "the reality of you is even better than the fantasy."

He pins my hips in place and fucks me harder. Every thrust makes my breath hitch, and my hands tighten around his shoulders, my nails digging in. But he holds me up easily. God, he's fucking strong. Did I know he was this strong?

With every thrust his cock drives deep into me, and it feels as though he's splitting me in two, perfectly so. My clit was already so swollen, my body so close to the edge, my pussy slick, that the press of his cock, the drag of his slightly curved tip in just the right place, just over that sensitive spot, is enough to make my toes curl in record time.

"I'm going... to come," I manage. My whole body is trembling, right on the edge of it.

Easton smiles. That slow, searing smile that drives me wild every time. "Good."

He leans in to kiss my neck and bites down lightly, right as he drives into me again. I cry out as the orgasm hits me. My pussy convulses around Easton's shaft, gripping him like a fist, as a wave of pleasure rocks through my body. I lose my grip on Easton's shoulder, but it doesn't matter. He's got me firmly in his arms, and he doesn't let go. He doesn't stop thrusting either, moving faster now, driving so hard into me I hear his balls slapping against me, and before long, I feel pressure building inside me again, right behind my navel, deep.

It's not possible I can come again. It can't be. It cannot—

The denial is ripped from my thoughts when I shatter.

Easton leans back just far enough to meet my gaze, enjoying the sight. "What about now?" he murmurs. "Does this count as losing control?"

CHAPTER 15

EASTON

A throbbing sensation in my cock wakes me the next morning. It only takes a split second to see why. Beside me in the bed, nestled in the crook of my arm, is Phoebe, stark naked. Her ass is pressed up against my hips, and I'm already rock hard.

That explains the wet dream. Or... wet memory?

Just the thought of last night is enough to make me groan. The lingerie I tore off her body. The wall I pinned her against, the sensation of release when I finally fucked the woman I've been dreaming about for weeks—my own wife.

And after that, I carried her upstairs, straight into my walk-in shower. I rubbed soap into her back, her long lean legs, her taut arms. Her hips, her ass, her breasts... By the time we got to the rinsing stage, she was trembling like a leaf. I could have done anything I wanted to her, but instead I pulled her into my arms and let my hand slip between her legs. Made her scream with pleasure all over again.

My cock gives an aching throb, and as if in answer, Phoebe wriggles in her sleep, her ass rubbing against my shaft.

Fuck. I can't take much more of this.

I slide one arm down from where I draped it around her waist and trace circles along her hipbone, the curve of her belly. Down across her soft mound, until my fingertips circle her clit, ever so lightly. Brushing back and forth until Phoebe wriggles again and lets out a sleepy little moan that nearly does me in.

How can I *still* want her this badly? Normally I get women out of my system in a night or two. Don't get me wrong, morning after sex is always on the table, but... there's usually not such a desperate edge to it. I feel like I didn't even fuck her at all.

You just haven't done it enough, I reassure myself. A few more times and I'll feel sated, as always.

I press a little harder against her clit, and Phoebe's lips part with a sigh. Her eyelids flutter, and she glances over her shoulder at me.

"Good morning to you too," she murmurs.

The half-smile on her face makes me want to thrust inside her already, watch her face come alive with want, the way it did last night when she came for me. But I have more self-control than that.

I slip my hand lower, pressing between her thighs to

trace the edges of her pussy lips. Then I grin. "Seems like someone was dreaming about me."

I press until my fingertip eases between her lips. I can already feel how wet she is, dripping along her inner thigh, pooling there. I trace my finger up the length of her slit and back down, slowly.

In response, she arches her hips to press her ass against my cock more firmly, smirking. "Pot, kettle."

"Never said I was complaining."

I kiss the nape of her neck, and she lets her eyes flutter shut again. She pushes back against me as I use my hand to spread her thighs and slide my cock between her legs. She shivers a little and clenches her thighs around my shaft. I part my lips to nip her neck lightly.

"You feel incredible already, and I'm not even inside you," I murmur, knowing my breath will feel hot against her neck where I just kissed her.

"Mm, guess you'd better rectify that." She peers at me again from beneath those lashes, over her shoulder.

Who could say no? Normally I'd want to draw this out more, tease her. Spend a little time tying her up or blindfolding her. But the ache has been building for too long. I twist to reach for my nightstand and the condoms I keep there. But Phoebe catches my wrist with one hand, arching a brow.

"Since we aren't sleeping with anyone else," she says slowly, "and I'm on the pill..."

"It's up to you," I reply, letting my hand draw back to trace her shoulder, her hip. I follow her hipbone arch down to the crease of her thigh. She shifts, both legs rubbing around either side of my cock, and I barely manage to suppress a groan.

Phoebe grins. "I want you inside me. Raw."

Jesus Christ. "Has anyone ever told you you've got a filthy mouth?"

With my mouth still on hers, I part her thighs and angle my hips. Then I break the kiss and gently bend her hips back until I can ease my cock between her soaking wet lips. Position the tip against her dripping pussy.

She moans against my mouth and breaks away just far enough to catch my eye. "One or two people might have mentioned it."

Challenge flares in my gut, my chest. "I'll just have to make sure you forget about them then." I want her all to myself. Entirely.

The possessive urge surprises me. Normally I'm happy to share—fewer strings attached that way. But then again, I've never fucked my actual wife before. Maybe that's why it's different.

I ease farther into her, inch by inch, savoring the way her walls clench around me, her pussy somehow slick and tight at the same time. I need her restrained, just a little. I need to feel her writhe.

"I forgot about them already."

I take her arms and pin them over her head by the wrists.

"Oh," she breathes so quietly I might have imagined it. "Yes."

She pushes her hips back into mine, and I'm back in the moment, not considering words anymore. Not considering anything but the feel of this warm, soft woman pressed into me, my cock driving into and out of her again, our bodies becoming slick with sweat. I hold her hands in place. She pushes and pulls, but I put my weight on them. I have her. She's in place. She's mine.

I lose track of everything except Phoebe's soft moans, the way they build toward louder, more desperate cries the harder and faster I fuck her, the tighter I hold her when the force of her orgasm hits.

I come not long after her, driving deep into her as it hits me. I feel my cum pumping into her, feel her pussy clenching around me, and only then do I wonder if I'm not the only one feeling sensations I'm not used to.

I fall back against the sheets, watch her twist around and do the same, both of us spread out in my oversized, larger-than-a-king bed.

"Am I crazy, or is it not usually this good?" I murmur, watching her from the corner of my eye.

Phoebe's eyes dart to mine, then away again, as though she's surprised. Surprised I said it? Or surprised I'm thinking the same thing she is?

She stares at the ceiling for a moment, then she forces a light, easy smile. Her usual one. I'm beginning to recognize it for what it really is—her favorite mask. "It's just new, that's all. Mark my words, we'll be through the whole sexual repertoire in, like, three weeks, and then this buzz will fade and we'll get over each other."

So she feels the buzz too. I smirk, lifting an eyebrow. "That sounds like a challenge, Mrs. Taylor."

She holds up a finger. "First of all, it's Mrs. Jones.

Never said I was taking your last name." She holds up another finger. "And secondly, what if it is?" She arches a brow too, mirroring me.

I laugh. "Let's agree on Jones-Taylor. And three weeks of material, that's all you think I've got? You're on. I've got *years'* worth." I'm sure I do, but I've never really thought about it.

I do, don't I?

"Well, you only have to make it through one year, no repeats."

As Phoebe meets my eye and sticks out a hand, like we're striking another deal, I think I might need to make some flash cards of my own. But for now, I push her hand away and flip her around until she's underneath me. From there, I kiss my way down her neck and along her collarbone.

We'll see who gets over who here…

CHAPTER 16

PHOEBE

I let out a little groan as I ease myself into the pedicure chair. Beside me, already situated in his seat, feet bubbling in a pool of warm water and a glass of champagne in hand, Monty arches a brow.

"Too much yoga?" he asks with a knowing little smirk.

I lean back and press the massage function on the back of the chair, letting it drag across my muscles as the woman doing my pedicure fills the tub with hot bubbles. "More like too much of my husband."

Monty's eyes light up. "Are you *finally* banging him?"

Our pedicurists exchange side-eyes, and I bite the inside of my lip. Surely they've heard weirder gossip working here, at one of the fanciest salons in Manhattan. The prices are so high that unlimited drinks come *free*.

That alone seems like it must come with a non-disclosure clause.

Still, I feel a little self-conscious as I shift in the massage chair, trying to get a kink out of my spine. "No, Monty, I'm not *banging* my husband. Banging is what George Lapras did to my cervix in senior year. This is…" I shut my eyes with a groan as the massage chair hits a particularly tight knot.

It sends me flashing back to last night. Actually, all of the last two weeks really. It's like since Easton and I finally broke the seal, we cannot keep our hands off one another. We've been working our way through rooms in the house—not to mention positions. Bent over the coffee table, or me perched on the kitchen counter. Me going down on him on the upstairs balcony, with a view out over Central Park as the sun rises. We probably gave some perv with binoculars a bigger show than they expected, but what the hell. It kind of added to it.

But last night was a new one for me. Last night was Easton blindfolding me with his tie and restraining my hands to either side of his bed. First came what I assume was a feather, somehow torturous and thrilling at the same time as he ran it over my naked limbs, my bare stomach, up my inner thighs. Then an ice cube against my navel, so cold I gasped, until he sucked it out and replaced it with his tongue, which felt white hot in contrast. Then he moved lower and lower, until he had his whole face pressed between my thighs, and—

Monty snaps his fingers in front of my face, bringing

me back to reality with a sigh. "That good? Damn, okay, Easton." Monty cackles.

I groan and swat Monty's arm. "Shut up. Marriage sex is crazy. I had no idea."

"Pretty sure marriage sex is boring and repetitive," Monty replies. "Straight marriage anyway. At least, so I hear."

I snort. "So far, not at all. Actually, we've got a bit of a bet going."

"Do tell."

"I told him he'd go through his entire repertoire in three weeks tops. He bet me he can go all year without a repeat."

Monty arches his eyebrows. "Like, physical position or...?"

"Whole situation." I gesture, thinking but not saying, *ropes, toys, swings.* Easton hasn't told me whether he owns a sex swing, but after seeing mere glimpses of his kinky side, it wouldn't surprise me. Also, if he doesn't, he might be getting one as, like, a six-month anniversary present. "Still, there's no way someone can go a whole *year* without repeating anything. I figure once we work our way through his every move, then I'll be able to stop wondering. Curiosity will be sated, and I can get back to focusing on my thesis."

I close my eyes and sink into the chair as my pedicurist works on my feet. When I open my eyes again, Monty is watching me strangely, an unreadable expression on his usually wide-open face.

"What?" I ask.

"You really think repeating one sexual position is going to suddenly let you concentrate on *writing a thesis* over fucking your incredibly hot husband?"

"You don't?" I fire back. "You just said married sex is boring and repetitive."

"Well, clearly I was underestimating how proactive you're being about preventing that." Monty smirks. "You've got to admit, that whole bet of yours sounds pretty fucking hot."

"Ugh." I fall back in my seat with a groan. "You're hopeless. First you berate me for not fucking my husband and now you want me to *keep* doing it... Have you no regard for my academic success?"

"It's called multitasking. Look it up." Monty swats my arm.

I brush him away, but I can't help laughing as I do.

"Speaking of academics." When I look back, Monty's eyes are alight all over again with some new mischief. "I know you're booked up this year, between wifely duties and school. but what about a little post-graduation trip? It'd be good to have something to look forward to..."

Post-graduation. Next summer. I can barely even think about next week, let alone that far ahead. There's way too much I need to sort out between then and now —finishing this semester, nailing my thesis next semester. Somehow surviving this whole marriage situation. And, by that date, I realize...

My gut tenses.

By next summer, the whole marriage thing will be

over. I'll be a young divorcee, freshly wealthy and without a care in the world.

Without Easton either.

I swallow around a sudden, unexpected lump. I'm only feeling this way because of all the hot sex. And because Easton isn't as big of a dick as I'd assumed. But that's all. By this time next spring, we'll be sick of each other and I'll be eager to move onto some new and exciting fling.

"Sure, I guess," I finally reply, realizing Monty is still waiting, though I barely process what I'm saying.

He lets out a whoop. "Great, because I found this amazing Groupon deal. Ten-day Hawaii trip, flights included. It's good for next June or July, so I figure when we get closer to, we can pick dates, live up the tropical single life to celebrate your freedom again."

I force myself to smile even wider. "Yeah. Freedom. That sounds perfect."

I meet Monty's eyes and hold his gaze, refusing to let him—or more importantly me—feel any sort of doubt about how I'll be feeling in nine months' time. How has it already been three months? My stomach churns. The year is a quarter gone already.

"Let's book it today," I insist.

Because Monty's right. Having something to look forward to will be good.

A good reminder to keep my feet on solid ground.

CHAPTER 17

EASTON

The Murray Loft is packed tonight. This is why I try to avoid the place on weekends—it's a completely different, and much louder, crowd. But Max and Dylan insisted, and when they started berating me about how long it's been since I met them to do anything besides running in the park or grabbing a quick lunch between work shifts, I caved. Maybe because they both made whip-cracking noises at me. But still. I'm not whipped by my fake wife's real pussy.

For some reason, I have to keep reminding myself to add the *fake* more and more often lately.

Maybe because of all the sex. Probably that. Just sitting on a corner barstool in a packed bar makes me think about all the other things I could be doing back at home. In fact, I've got to cover my phone screen so no one sees the half a dozen new positions I've been googling for ideas, almost all of which involve Phoebe and little to no clothing.

For a moment, I picture her a couple of days ago, kneeling on the balcony outside my bedroom, her eyes fixed on mine as she wrapped those perfect, plump lips around the head of my cock. And the way she looked after she finally relaxed and let me take control, loosening her jaw so my rod reached all the way to the back of her throat... Her eyes watered, but she didn't look away from me. She hadn't stopped moaning either, and the vibrations that added ...

"Hello? Refill?" Dylan waves a hand in front of my face.

I startle back to reality. The deafening bar-turned-pseudo-club. My friends smirking at me.

"Yes," I say too quickly, and shove my empty glass in Dylan's direction.

He flags down the bartender—not the one Phoebe's friends with, I note, but an older, grumpier looking guy.

Unlike Dylan, Max isn't as easily distracted. He grabs my phone without so much as a warning and tilts the screen to squint at it. "What is this, Phoebe-Sutra?" He snorts and slides the phone back to me. "Seriously? Mister Kink-of-the-Week ran out?"

"Never get married," I reply, deadpan. "Not even fake married. Next thing you know, your wife is demanding that you keep it fresh or she's going to leave—and let me tell you, I *thought* I had plenty of material, but when you're fucking two or three times a day..."

Max is still cackling when Dylan turns back with

fresh glasses of whiskey for all three of us. I take mine and toss half of it back in one go, even though it's definitely a sipping scotch. The burn helps me think a little straighter.

Dylan smirks. "I told you you'd get into trouble if you went through with this."

I glare at him. "Did you though? Because all *I* remember is you making bets about it."

"Right. I bet it would end in disaster."

"Actually," Max cuts in, "you bet she would get way too attached and our boy here would have to deal with a whole mess when it came time to extricate his dick." He scratches his chin. "Neither of us bet *Easton* would get attached…"

"I'm not *attached*."

"Literally?" Max arches a brow. "You were just bitching about how often you have to fuck your wife so she won't leave you."

"No, I was bitching about the different *ways* I have to —you know what, shut up." I scowl, and it only deepens when my two best friends burst into laughter. They are the absolute worst. "Look, our arrangement is only a quarter finished. I have to keep living with this woman for another nine months." *Christ, is it only nine already?* I push that thought from my mind and ignore a strange tightening sensation in my chest. "There's no reason not to keep her happy. Less of a headache for me. Plus, I mean, sex is sex."

"Who could have predicted?" Max shoots a look at Dylan, and they snicker.

Dylan is the first to sober up again. "Hey, man, seriously though. A situation like this has danger: flammable written all over it. Don't get burned, okay?"

Now it's my turn to laugh. "Okay, Grandma. Thanks for the tip."

"I mean it. You've never had your heart broken, right? Take it from me, it sucks."

Something in Dylan's expression makes me wonder what I've missed. We talk about most things. Women, work, vacations. But heartbreak? I never thought Dylan had that in his past.

Before I can ask, Max elbows me back into the conversation. "Please. This is Easton we're talking about. He's fireproof, right?" Max slaps my shoulder, and I force my usual, easy grin. It doesn't feel so easy right now.

"Exactly," I agree, though deep down, my insides are screaming anything but.

On my phone, still lying faceup on the bar top where Max slid it, the Kama Sutra listicle stares up at me, a series of cartoon figures fucking in various and increasingly improbable-looking knots. All I can think about is what happens when I run out of ideas. When Phoebe gets bored. When my house goes back to being the big, fancy, clean, designer space I built, instead of the zany, cat-shredded, messy *home* it's starting to feel like.

My fists bunch. But it's not my friends I'm pissed at anymore. It's myself. Because they're right.

I'm about to get burned.

CHAPTER 18

PHOEBE

We're three months into our fake union when Easton decides it's time for me to meet the work colleagues. Officially anyway. I saw a few of them on my brief unannounced trip to his office, but that hardly counts. And apparently Grandma Sofia (my absolute fave) has been asking about me, wondering why Easton hasn't brought me to any functions.

She even went so far as to send flowers to Easton's house, on a weekday in the middle of the afternoon when she must have known I'd be the only person home. The card tied to the beautiful bouquet read: *If Easton has ordered you to stay away from the office, you have my permission to poison his dinner,* along with a hand-drawn heart.

Naturally, I showed Easton the flowers the minute he got home, cackling the whole time.

His response was to agree that he would indeed lock

me in here, and himself with me, if he thought he could get away with it. Then he threw me over his shoulder and carried me upstairs, only to toss me onto his bed and pull my legs up over his shoulders, my hips arched underneath him so he had easy access to thrust into me from below...

I've got to say, his positions are getting even *more* creative as time goes on, not less.

What am I going to do if he doesn't run out of material soon? I mean, besides enjoy the ride obviously.

I'm still thinking far too much about riding my husband when Norm drops me off outside the upscale fancy restaurant with a Japanese name I'm not even going to attempt pronouncing. Easton is waiting outside for me, in the middle of a crowd of suits that I would normally mock, or at least steer clear of. But instead, just one glimpse of his dark hair, effortlessly tousled over one eye in a way that I now know for a fact is completely legit, not just feigned casual, makes my heart skip.

Then it pounds, when he spots the car and comes over to open the door for me.

"Bye, Norm," I call as I slide out.

Norm gives me a cheerful wave, calling at us both to have fun before he drives off. Easton, meanwhile, is staring at me with an intense scrutiny that makes my cheeks feel hot.

"What?" I ask.

But he breaks into a smile and offers his arm. "You look nice."

"*Nice?*" I narrow my eyes playfully, but loop my arm

through his all the same. "*Nice* is a compliment for your sister or your grandma."

"My apologies." He smirks and leans in close, his lips grazing my ear, voice a low whisper. "Seeing you in that dress makes me want to tug you into a bathroom and fuck you until you're screaming my name."

When he pulls away, my blush has only gotten worse, and this bastard knows it.

"Better?" he asks.

Then we reach his circle of coworkers—coworkers!—and I'm forced to swallow any kind of retort. Which is good, because for once, I find myself tongue-tied and out of a quick retort. I manage to swallow, barely, then I'm being introduced.

I remember a few names: Easton's secretary, Anna, an older woman who compliments my shoes, which makes me like her immediately; Ryan and Jack, two brown-haired white guys who have got to be either siblings or products of such similar family environments that they came out looking nigh on identical; Beth, the only other woman around my age; and three older men whose names all start with S, which seems like cheating, because now I can't remember any of them.

The restaurant host escorts us to our table—which turns out to be a private room in what looks like a tradi-tional Japanese-style house, complete with sliding bamboo doors, mats on the ground, and when we reach the dinner table, pillows for chairs.

"Um," I say, because my dress is mid-thigh length on a good day.

Easton bites his cheek in a way that I've come to recognize as his "trying not to laugh" face. I elbow him when nobody's looking, and he leans in, his breath hot and distracting.

"Much as I'd enjoy the show, I can't say I want to share *that* much of my wife with anybody," he says.

I think that's all, but then I feel something pressed into my hands. I look down and realize he's handed me his suit jacket. It's somehow both hot and sweet at the same time.

I wait until the others have taken their seats—how does everyone manage to kneel and sit on the floor so gracefully in suits and dresses?—before I awkwardly fumble into mine, Easton's coat draped over my lap so nobody can see when my skirt rides up.

Easton takes the pillow beside mine, and without missing a beat, he slides his hand under the suit jacket to rest, his palm searing hot against my inner thigh, mere inches from the edge of my panties. I swallow hard against a spike in my pulse. It's going to be a long dinner.

Across the table, Easton's secretary is beaming at me. "So…" She leans forward on two elbows, for all the world reminding me of my own grandmother when she used to badger me for gossip about my parents. The unexpected memory makes me smile. "How did you two meet?"

On cue, the rest of the table falls silent, and a half dozen faces eagerly swivel in my direction.

"Actually—" Easton starts, but I cut him off.

"At Freddy's," I interject. "Maybe you know it? It's in Brooklyn."

The old S-named guys all nod, and Beth, the one woman in a suit, flashes me a smile.

"That place is my favorite," she says, though I can't tell from her tone if she's being serious or trying to help me out.

Either way, I appreciate it. I smile back and shrug. "Easton just came up out of the blue and turned on the charm. And from there, well..."

"It was worldwindy," Easton says, his voice loud enough to reach everybody, though I feel like it's really just for me.

I stifle a smile as the S-names trade confused glances, and Ryan murmurs, *"Does he mean whirlwind?"* in a not-so-sotto voce to Jack.

Thankfully, a server intervenes then to brief us on the meal we'll be having. Some kind of preset menu, which I'm half grateful for because I'm in no mood to make decisions, but also a little bit annoyed about. Shouldn't a place this fancy let you pick what you want?

But I forgive them when the first course turns out to be the best salad I've ever had, some kind of taro and dandelion mix (who knew?) topped with a mind-blowing dressing and paired with miso soup that has way more veggies than I'm used to.

"This beats the hell out of Sushi Palace," I murmur to Easton, while the others are talking about quarterly returns or some other mind-numbing work stuff.

He flashes me a grin. "Wait until we get to the sashimi course."

"Is that the one that's all fish no rice?" I ask dubiously.

But when the sashimi course arrives—a series of fish slices so delicate and fresh they practically melt on my tongue, barely tasting like fish at all—I realize I had nothing to worry about.

"Is *this* why rich people are always obsessing about Japan?" I ask Easton, but I guess my voice carries farther than I expect.

"Have you ever been?" one of the S-names interjects, with a bright-eyed, anticipatory glow I've come to recognize from years in the service industry. "It's incredible."

I can barely keep the amusement out of my voice. "No, I've never been to Japan. Never been out of the country actually. Though I'm going to Hawaii next summer," I add, wanting to sound a little more cultured. And thanking the hell out of Monty and his Groupon at the same time.

Now every head swivels my way again. Including Easton's.

"Whaaat?" ask several other people.

"You haven't taken her to Paris?" Beth rolls her eyes at Easton.

He doesn't seem to notice. He's studying me closely, with an unreadable expression.

"Pfft. Paris smells like shit half the year," one of the lookalike guys—Jack or Ryan, I've had enough wine I can no longer remember—replies.

"Everyone's going to Croatia now," the other lookalike replies. "Better beaches."

"Admit it, you're just a *Game of Thrones* stan," Beth accuses, which makes me like her even more, especially when both lookalikes sputter in response.

"What's a stan?" asks one of the older S-names.

I think I'm in the clear, but then Anna, who's been watching Easton and me far too closely for comfort, jumps in.

"So is Easton taking you to Hawaii for your honeymoon?" Anna asks with a grin that Easton's whip-sharp grandmother would've been proud of. "You haven't used your vacation days in half a decade, Easton Taylor."

"Oh, we… haven't really talked honeymoons," Easton replies, shaking himself out of whatever stupor he entered since he heard me mention Hawaii.

"Well, Maui's a good start," one of the S-named men says. "You've sure been plenty of times."

"Though I hope you're not taking her to that God-awful resort they put us up in for the convention last time," another S-name mutters, and everyone is distracted by work talk again.

Which leaves me free to study the expression on Easton's face. He pushes his current course—a bamboo, tofu, and fava bean dish that is making me rethink every judgy comment I've ever made about vegetarian food in my life—around his plate without taking so much as a bite.

Across the table, Anna catches my eye and smiles reassuringly. "You know, my husband and I didn't take a trip together until we'd been married for five years. When we finally did though, oh, it was lovely. And we've been married for thirty-five more years since, so he must agree." She chuckles.

"Where did you go?" I ask, genuinely interested. Not just in the trip, but in her whole situation. Married for forty years, but she doesn't sound cynical when she talks about her husband. She lights up as though she's still... well... *into* him. It's cute.

It makes me wonder if that sort of thing could really be possible. Still feeling someone after all that time. *Not getting repetitive.* The thought makes me steal another sideways glance at Easton, who's still avoiding my eye.

"Hawaii, actually." Anna's smile widens. "But not Maui. Kauai. It's got some of the most beautiful scenery you've ever seen in your entire life. Never mind beaches—the jungles there, hiking up through some of the most breathtaking forests you've ever seen. Not sure what itinerary you two have planned, but you should include it." Anna winks.

I follow her gaze to Easton, who finally looks at me. There's something unreadable in his gaze, distant and closed off in a way I've never seen before.

"Definitely," he says, more to Anna than me. Then he turns back to his plate and actually eats.

I shift on my cushion, uncomfortable. And I notice that for the first time since we sat down, Easton has moved away from me. His side isn't touching mine, and his hand isn't resting on my leg. His absence, though he's only sitting a couple feet away, makes me feel... empty somehow. Colder than I was before.

The rest of the meal progresses easily enough. Mostly

everyone talks business, though Anna makes an effort to loop me in now and then, trying to explain the various intricacies of their office politics. I try to pay attention, but it's hard when my gaze keeps looping back to Easton and his broody expression.

Normally he's so chatty and readable like an open book.

By the time the meal ends, my irritation has crescendoed into full-blown annoyance. I wait until we're out on the curb, waiting for the hired car Easton called, since Norm is off at this hour. The others have all dispersed by now, some to the subway and some in cabs. Finally, I can't take it any longer.

"What is it?" I blurt.

He meets my eye, which at least is an improvement. But then he raises an eyebrow like he doesn't understand. "What is what?"

"Something is obviously bothering you. You've been moody ever since Anna asked about honeymoons. Is that the problem? Because we never wrote a honeymoon or anything into the contract; don't worry, I don't expect a free trip from you."

Easton's expression, if possible, only hardens further. "I'm not moody."

"Oh sure, that tone is extremely convincing."

"You just never mentioned you were going to Hawaii." He shrugs.

I cross my arms. "Because it's happening after—" I cut myself off before I add the words "we break up." We both know exactly what after means. "Besides I only *just* made those plans. Also, since when are you my keeper?"

He groans. "I never said I was—nor would I want to be."

Ouch, I think, but then I wonder, *why?* I've always valued my freedom, so why would it annoy me that he dismisses this idea so quickly? *Nor would I want to be* rankles at me though.

"Just you said summer," he says. "So I wasn't sure about timing."

Oh. Now I get it.

"Don't worry." I step toward him, trying on my best reassuring expression. "It wouldn't be until June or July. After..." I clear my throat and wonder why it's hard to force out the words. "After you get your full twelve months."

"Ah."

I thought that would mollify him. But if anything, he looks more irritated now. Just then, our hired care pulls up, and he flags it down with a raised fist.

"Easton, what is it? Seriously."

"Nothing. If you want to go to Hawaii in June, great. None of my business. We won't be together anymore."

My stomach could sink all the way down through the subway grate we're standing over right now. "Right. Great. Cool."

He yanks open the door of the car and gestures for me to get in first. We don't speak again until we pull away from the curb, both of us glaring out of our own separate windows.

"You do know we'll have to act upset when we split up, right?"

I side-eye him. "Is that why you're upset? It'll look bad if your ex-wife goes to Hawaii too soon after the divorce? Because I can send your grandma a whole bunch of moody texts while I'm there if it helps. Or maybe just refer her to every post-breakup romcom about how to recover from heartbreak..."

"I'm sure that will be really convincing," he replies, deadpan.

I swallow hard and stare out my side of the car at the passing Manhattan streetlights. Then an idea strikes. I open my purse and root through it for the stack of index cards I keep with me so I can quiz myself on subway rides or while I'm waiting for spin class to start. Most are filled with glossary terms of things I have to memorize. At the back of the stack, however, I find a blank card and wriggle it free. I grab a pen next and click it open.

In the window reflection, I see Easton shift in his seat. He peers over at me, without trying to seem like he's interested in what I'm doing.

I write in big block letters anyway, so he can see.

DEALS WITH STRESS BY:

Then I hold the card up facing him, a silent question.

Parenthetical lines appear on either side of his mouth. He's repressing a smile now, I can tell. "Working out."

I jot down the answer on the back of the card, suppressing a smile of my own.

But then he adds, "And eating a shit-ton of ice cream."

My hand freezes, pen still gripped in it. I do the same thing.

Without meeting his gaze, I crumple the card in my fist and turn to face my car window again, praying my expression remains blank and unreadable.

Neither of us speak the rest of the ride home.

CHAPTER 19

EASTON

Phoebe doesn't come upstairs the way she normally would after showering and changing on her own floor. I pace around my bedroom, unable to get our conversation out of my mind. This whole Hawaii thing has thrown me. I didn't realize she was already making plans for next year. And not just twelve months from now but... after.

But of course she is. That's the whole point of this arrangement, isn't it? She helps me secure my position at the company, and I help her graduate and start her career without debts. It's only natural she'd want to take a trip to celebrate that.

It's not Phoebe's fault that the mental image of her celebrating in Hawaii mere weeks after we divorce puts a rock in my gut.

No. Actually, it's the thought of the word "divorce" in the first place.

Now we're fighting because of something that isn't even going to happen for three-quarters of a year. I remind myself to live in the present, but I'm not that guy. I'm not the "Be Here Now" dude in tie-dye with humming bowls. I don't even own incense.

Living in the present is for guys who don't care about the future, and the whole point of this endeavor is the future. My future. At my family company.

Phoebe and I still have eight and a half months together left. That's more than enough time for me to get over these impractical emotions. Not to mention I still have plenty of my repertoire left to work through. We agreed we wouldn't get bored of one another until we started repeating things—that has to be why I'm so moody at the thought of her Hawaiian trip. Because we haven't reached the boredom stage yet.

Only one way to get there.

I square my shoulders and head downstairs. Phoebe is still in her bathroom on the second floor, but the door is open wide enough for me to see she's wearing a white T-shirt that ends at mid thigh. She's bent close to the mirror, swabbing at her face with makeup remover.

Just the sight of her bent at that angle is enough to drive any inconvenient emotions out of my mind, replacing them with entirely more welcome thoughts. Memories of the last time I bent her over this bathroom counter, for starters.

I nudge the door open. It creaks as it goes, and Phoebe glances at me in the mirror.

"There is one other way I deal with stress," I tell her,

thinking about the index card she crumpled earlier, when she thought I wasn't looking.

She blinks once, twice. Turns back to the mirror and swabs off the last of her mascara before she tosses the tissue into the garbage can. "What's that?"

I step into the bathroom. Approach slowly. She watches me in the mirror, not commenting. Not telling me to fuck off either, which seems like progress. When I reach her, I slide an arm around her shoulders, tug her against my side, and meet her gaze in the mirror with a sly half-smile.

"Well, for starters, I picture you in that lacy bra you wore the first time you ambushed me in the living room. Do you remember?"

She stifles a smile, clearly annoyed with herself for it. "I *ambushed* you, did I?"

"Definitely." I trace my hand from her shoulder down to her elbow and back up. I barely touch her, light enough that I can see the goose bumps that rise in the wake of my fingertips, the fine hairs standing on end. "I was the innocent, unsuspecting victim of that seduction."

She snorts. "*Innocent*, sure. You do remember you showed me your toy collection last week, right?"

I arch a brow. "Would you like to browse it again, Mrs. Taylor-Jones?"

She presses her lips together. *Definitely* struggling not to grin now. "That depends, Mr. Taylor-Jones." She raises her chin, as if daring me to contradict the hyphen. "Do you have a new use for said toys to show me?"

"Just one? So little faith in me, wife."

Without another word, I catch her by the waist and hoist her over my shoulder. Phoebe lets out a startled shout, but she's laughing too as she feigns swatting my backside with both hands.

"You're a caveman."

"You like it," I reply firmly, and I take the shiver that passes through her for agreement.

I toss her onto my bed, but before she can get far, I lean over to pin her underneath me, my hands wrapped around her wrists. She grins up at me, and that smirk alone almost undoes me, because it's so unlike any other woman I've been with.

"You realize we've already checked off missionary, right?" she murmurs, leaning up to kiss me.

I catch her mouth with mine, parting her lips, my tongue sliding between hers as I claim her mouth. Already, I feel the hard throb of my cock where it digs into that flat plane of her belly. She shifts beneath me, and I know she feels it too. I hear the hitch in her breathing, feel her chest rise and fall faster against mine as I break the kiss, leaning back to drink in the sight of her.

"Oh, I know," I reply. "I'm not finished yet."

It takes her a second to catch her breath, which is gratifying. Even more so when I reach over her and behind the bed to tug free a long length of velvety strap, and her breath catches.

"You love your restraints," she murmurs, an answering heat already visible in her gaze.

"And you love being at my mercy."

I dip to kiss her again and she arches up to meet me, but I turn at the last moment, running my tongue and the edges of my teeth along her jawline, her neck, down to cross her collarbone. She shivers, and the sensation alone is delicious. Her body softens in anticipation, and when I tongue the right spot at the crook of her neck, she lets out a breathy little moan, as I knew she would.

I admit, there might be something to fucking the same woman for longer than a brief fling. It's gratifying to know her this well, to already anticipate how she'll respond to every touch. It's anything but boring. With Phoebe, it's like a challenge I can't see ever getting tired of.

But then I think about what she said the first night we hooked up. How sure she was that we'd get boring and repetitive before long, and my ambition to prove her wrong is fired up all over again.

"Turn over," I command.

Phoebe raises a brow but does as I say, twisting herself around beneath me, her body pressing up against mine all the while and nearly driving me mad. "We also did doggie-style two weeks ago."

"Put your hands behind your back," I reply, and I'm rewarded by another little shiver that she tries and fails to disguise.

She puts her hands at the small of her back. I reach around her and pull the front of her shirt over her head and drag it over her arms, binding them together behind her.

"Okay. Maybe not *this* doggie-style," she says with a grin.

"God, you are fucking sexy as hell."

"You've mentioned that once or twice," she says.

I pull her hips up until her knees are under her and her bottom's high enough to reach. "Speaking of what I mentioned, let's talk about things you neglected to mention."

"Like?" Her cheek is on the sheets and her suspicious look comes through a nest of messy hair.

"Like... Hawaii."

"It's not like you ran your post-divorce itinerary by me either."

Divorce. What's with that word? Why does she keep using it? With a *thwack,* I spank her bottom. Not even hard, so her gasp must be surprise.

"You're getting one slap for everything you're going to do in Hawaii you didn't tell me about."

I move her hair away to make sure she's all right. She sticks her tongue out at me.

Yeah. She's fine.

"Start talking, Phoebe."

"Or what?"

I slide my fingertips along her seam, barely touching her. It's not reward time yet. Not until she knows she's going to have a shitty time in Hawaii without me.

"Or I'm going to bed and leaving you here with your hands tied where they can't reach your wet little pussy."

"You wouldn't."

I shrug and start to get off the bed.

"Scuba diving!" she cries.

"Good girl." I slap her right butt cheek. "What else?"

She bites her lip and considers her next words. "Para-sailing."

When I hit the same spot again, just a little harder, a pink spot rises. God, I love that as much as the way she bites her lip.

"Helicopter tour. Like *Magnum PI.*"

"You get one for the helicopter." I deliver it. "And this one..." I spank her a second time and she groans. "Is for bringing up an eighties TV show during sex."

"Whale watch." Spank. She writhes and moans. "Beach comb." I start on the left side and she yelps because it's unexpected. "Luau."

The left again. Her eyes flutter closed and her lips part. Then she looks at me with this particularly Phoebe-ish mischief.

"What?"

"Surf, paddleboard, camp, tour a volcano, swim, play golf, and that thing where you fly through the trees on a rope."

I spank her six times in quick succession and now her back is arched and she's gasping.

"It's called ziplining," I say, stroking her beautiful ass.

"You missed one."

"I don't believe you're going golfing." I kiss the pink patches on her ass, where the skin is still hot, and tease with my tongue, drawing a sigh of anticipation from her. "Why, Mrs. Taylor-Jones." I taste her, and she wiggles closer. "You seem to be quite excited about this trip."

I part her legs and kneel between them, positioned behind her prone form, as I trace a fingertip along the outer lips of her pussy. I've barely done more than spank her. I never thought she'd go for it in the first place, much less get *this* wet.

"What can I say? My husband is sending me off with a memory for each activity," Phoebe murmurs, and just the sound of those words, *my husband*, sends another throb of desire straight to my already stiff cock.

"Fuck, Phoebe." I kiss her tied hands, then bite her ass where it's pink just hard enough to make her laugh and squirm. "You like it."

I nudge her knees farther apart and press my face between them, running my tongue along the length of her slit, pressing the tip between her folds, far enough that I can taste her juices, savor how wet she is for me already.

She lets out another soft sound, nearly a moan. "I like it."

"Good," I reply quietly before I lick her again, all the way to the end of her slit, my tongue circling her clit deftly before I slide back up, tracing the outline of her entrance. With my free hand, I part her pussy lips, and I wrap my other hand around one of her hips, my fingers digging in for purchase. Then, ever so slowly, I push the tip of my tongue inside her.

She moans louder, squirming against the bed. "Easton..."

I circle my tongue inside her, savoring the way she tastes, sweet and salty and just a hint musky. I love her flavor. I could spend all day here, savoring each taste of her. But I draw my tongue back out, dragging along her inner walls, before I push it back in again, faster.

She gasps, and her hips buck up off the bed, back toward me.

I keep going, teasing her inch by inch, my tongue alternating between penetrating her and circling her clit, not quite touching. Just adding enough pressure to drive her wild. When I sense she's nearing her peak, I draw back entirely, sitting up to gaze down at her naked body bent before me, every glorious, beautiful inch of her.

"*Fuck*, Easton," she breathes. "Fuck me, please…"

I grin. "Oh, I plan to."

But before I do, I reach across the bed for a pillow. I ease her hips up and prop the pillow beneath them, angling her hips just right. She arches her back, trying to press her hips against mine, but I pin her against the pillow with one hand while I get my dick out of my jeans with the other.

I'm rewarded by the searing heat in her gaze as she fixes it on me. I position myself at her entrance, tracing the head of my cock up and down her slit, coating myself in her juices, my eyes fixed on hers the whole time.

"Just fuck me already."

"I don't know," I tell her, grinning. "I'm not sure I'm convinced you can do all those activities in one vacation."

"I'm going to go on that hike that Anna woman mentioned too."

"Are you?"

"If you don't fuck me right now."

"Is that any way to talk to a guy who has you tied up?" I take her by the elbows and pull back, just for that extra measure of control.

"Please," she groans. "Please fuck me. I'll be nice."

"Atta girl." I ease inside her slowly, an inch at a time.

She stretches her legs wider to accommodate me and arches her back so her hips angle up toward mine. I keep going, so slowly it's probably driving us both wild, until my cock is fully inside her pussy and I feel her contracting, tightening around me.

"Your pussy was built for my cock, Phoebe." Pulling her arms back, I thrust hard, one time, and she cries out. "Your body loves being at my mercy."

"No mercy. Yes." Her last word emerges a gasp as I pull out of her and thrust back in, moving faster now.

I draw back again, thrust in once more, harder. She tries to move her hips with me, but in this position, I have all the control, and I take full advantage.

Letting go of her arms, I grip her hips, angling myself so that my cock presses deep inside her, running along her inner front wall. It doesn't take long before she's breathing faster, her body quivering on the edge. She was already so turned on, and I know exactly where to thrust by now to hit that sweet spot.

I fuck her harder, faster, feel the tip of my cock drag along her walls and her muscles contract around my shaft with each thrust. I'm still going strong when I feel her start to come undone.

"I'm going... to..." She can't even finish, and I grin.

"Come for me, wife."

Her whole body shakes as the orgasm hits her. I don't stop or even slow. I keep thrusting deep into her, our bodies making slick sounds where we collide. She lets out a faint cry, and it becomes a keening sound as I keep fucking her. I can't tell where her first orgasm ends and the next builds, but within minutes she's crying out again, her pussy contracting so hard around my cock it feels like a fist.

I come deep inside her, with a grunt so guttural it feels as though it's been pulled straight from my balls. Then I collapse to the sheets, pausing just long enough to untangle her shirt from her arms. She curls against my chest, both of us sticky with sweat, but our eyes wide open, fixed on each other.

She kisses me and I pull her against me, savoring the feel of her warm body against mine, her arms around my waist in the mirror image of the way mine curve around hers.

Lying like this, it's easy to forget why we were even fighting.

CHAPTER 20

PHOEBE

I'm late.

Not late for meeting a friend for lunch, late.

Late.

I count and recount the dates on the app on my phone, sure it must be wrong. I've been taking the pill for years now, at the same time every day. I'm usually regular as clockwork. But now, here it is in black-and-white—or rather, in the hot pink font this stupid period tracker app uses because I guess it thinks it will make the whole process of being female seem cute and fun, rather than a bloody mess.

My period is a week and a half late.

It could totally be nothing. Stress messes with your cycle, and God knows I've got plenty of that lately. Between my finals coming up in a few weeks, and my thesis being a vague collection of quotes and no actual *thesis* to tie the whole paper together yet—something my advisor reminds me literally every time I meet with her now—it's completely understandable my body would react.

However...

I can't stop thinking about the other possibility. I thought it would be fine to stop using condoms with Easton since I'm on the pill and we're both exclusive for the time being. Was that a mistake? Was this entire *mess* a mistake?

Oh God. Imagine if I do get pregnant. How could I explain this to a child? "Well, honey, your daddy really needed to trick your great-grandmommy into giving him something, and your mommy was a broke college student, so we decided to fake fall in love, and then along came you!"

Talk about a therapy-inducing start to life.

Roger winds around and around my ankles as I stand in my bathroom, scowling at my reflection. Then, when I don't bend down to pet him, he leaps onto the counter to headbutt me instead.

"Okay, okay." I scoop him into my arms and cuddle him close.

He purrs immediately and nuzzles my chin with his nose.

"What do you think?" I ask and bend to kiss that nose. He purrs even louder. "Would you like a baby brother or sister to torment?"

Roger squints at me as if to say, *no, I would not like to share my mother's doting affection.*

I sigh and set him on the counter again with one last long ear-scratch. "I know. It would be terrible timing. Plus, I mean, I don't even know if Easton *wants* kids. Or hell. If I do."

Roger tilts his head.

"You're right. I shouldn't stress until I know if it's even a thing."

Roger meows.

"You're so wise," I tell him.

But then he hops off the counter and bolts toward his food dishes, and I sigh.

"I already fed you, liar," I grumble, on my way past him and down the stairs.

There's one way to reassure myself. Otherwise, I'll waste the whole day obsessing about this.

I walk to the corner store and pick out the box labeled *Early Detection! One Simple Step! Know Now!* At the checkout, the older woman behind the counter offers me the weirdest half-smile ever, as though she isn't sure whether she should look congratulatory or consolatory. In return, I offer a weak shrug and swipe my card, then I hurry back to the house.

Roger is even more insistent that I should feed him again. I ignore his protestations and head straight for the bathroom. He, of course, follows me inside—why are cats such creepers about toilets? But there's something reassuring about Roger's familiar furry presence, literally perched on my lap as I wait for the results of the pee stick. I hold my breath and bury my face in his fur, mentally counting down the seconds until my phone alarm goes off.

For a moment, I don't move. Until I look at the pee stick, none of this is happening. Or not happening.

But finally, I can't avoid it any longer. I lift my head, pick up the stick, and...

No pink lines.

I let out a huge breath, one I didn't even realize I'd been holding. Then I'm hit with a wave of emotions that I really, really didn't know I was holding. Complicated emotions. Part relief, yes. But part... *disappointment?*

Do I *want* a baby?

More importantly, do I want *Easton's* baby?

Not right now. It would ultra-complicate an already complicated situation. But I think about how cute a little miniature Easton-and-me would be. He or she might have Easton's dark hair, his sharp features, my big eyes... hopefully my nose too, because Easton has a bit of a hook-nose thing going on. It totally works for him, but on a baby...

I shake my head, unsure why I'm smiling so hard at the thought of this.

And of course, a second later, that smile melts again, when it hits me. This is not a possibility. The mini-me part is, but the Easton-being-involved part? No way he'd go for having a kid with me. He doesn't even want to be in an actual *relationship* with me.

"This marriage is fake, Phoebe," I mutter, to remind myself.

In response, I stand up so abruptly that Roger goes

flying, and he lets out an angry meow before bolting under my bed.

"Sorry!" I call after him.

Then I scoop up the negative pregnancy test and toss it into the trash. I take the box it came in to my study room and root around until I find my flash cards. I set the empty test box on the dresser and start to write, mostly to clear my head.

REASONS THIS WOULD NEVER WORK:

On the backside, I find the list comes easily. *Easton never feeds Roger. Easton does not scoop the litter box. Easton would not change a diaper or feed a baby either. Easton would not allow a baby on his furniture. Easton doesn't do commitment. Easton doesn't want me.*

The last line is so pathetic that even I cringe at it. I let out a long sigh that turns into a groan and rip the card in half. Then I stuff it inside the pregnancy test box and shove it into my desk drawer alongside the other index cards, before I get ready to go to the gym and spin class. Anything to take my mind off this.

But the box, I'll save. It will be my reminder. Something to stare at any time I start to forget that the life I'm currently living—a life that feels more and more real by the day—is anything but.

CHAPTER 21

EASTON

Something has changed.

Not the sex, of course. That's still as hot as ever—which is to say, hotter than I ever imagined sex could be.

But ever since dinner out with my coworkers, Phoebe has seemed distant. We still talk, still joke, still run through lists of kinky new positions. But there's a space between us I never felt before. A distant, distracted look in her eye whenever we talk. And she hasn't mentioned Hawaii—or, in fact, anything about next year—since that night.

I know something is wrong. I must have done something wrong. Was it the spanking? Something during the meal? I can't quite figure it out.

Or maybe it's simpler than that, my brain can't help pointing out. Maybe she's just eager for her single-lady flings in Hawaii. Maybe, despite the fact that we haven't repeated a single position yet, she's already bored of me. Bored of marriage. Bored of our life together.

I shake off that anxious, doubting voice. I'm only going to make myself paranoid, and a paranoid me is no fucking fun. If Phoebe isn't already sick of me, she will be soon.

The question is, why do I care? Aren't I sick of her yet?

And that alone makes me realize that Phoebe isn't the only one being distant lately. If I'm being honest, I've been hiding from her a little bit too.

Because from the moment she brought up Hawaii, I started thinking about the *after* of all this: after our divorce, after we both go our separate ways... well, it's been a hell of a lot harder to keep my head in the present. I can't stop thinking about my friends warning me I'm going to get burned.

I can't stop worrying they're right.

But I have eight months left to go in this arrangement. Plenty of time to figure out my shit. In the meantime, I still have a moody wife to contend with, so when I wake up and find the house empty—except, of course, for Roger meowing pitifully beside his food dish—I decide I need to take matters into my own hands.

There's got to be some way to cheer her up...

Absently, I fill Roger's dish, the way I always do whenever Phoebe isn't here and the cat begs. Last thing I want is for her to accuse me of starving the poor creature. Roger rubs around my ankles in thanks, and after checking quickly over my shoulder to be sure Phoebe isn't lurking somewhere with a video camera, ready to film this for blackmail, I bend down and scratch his ear for a minute before I leave him to eat his meal.

Phoebe has been studying her ass off for her finals, but I know for a fact she hasn't started drafting her thesis yet. I also know that she prefers to write at her desk, but I've overheard her complaining to Monty on the phone about how the study has no natural light. It's a minor thing, but I figure I can rearrange the house a bit while she's out. After all, she'll have to spend a lot of time at her desk once she begins the writing process. And there's a free bedroom a few doors down, one I normally reserve for whenever my parents are visiting and my mom doesn't want to trek back to their crash pad after late dinners. It has more south-facing windows.

The spare room has a big patio with huge doors over-looking a similar view to my balcony upstairs, the one I know Phoebe loves. All it will take is a little bit of furniture shuffling, and I can give her the perfect new office.

If that doesn't cheer her up, I don't know what will.

In her current study, I carefully remove her laptop and electronics from the desk before I try to move it. Last thing I want to do is break something important. But when I try to slide the heavy oak desk, it sticks on the carpet. *Fuck.* This is heavier than I remember.

I'll have to take out the drawers.

I pull out the top one first, then each consecutive drawer. Most of them are filled with papers or candy— how many snacks does she need while she's working?

But in the bottom drawer, something catches my eye.

A box rolling around, cardboard but seemingly empty. Thinking it's trash, I pick it up, then freeze.

Early Detection! One Simple Step! Know Now!

A hard rock settles into my stomach. I've never seen one of these in person, but it's obvious what it is. A pregnancy test. And when I shake the box, something rattles inside it, making that rock climb up into my throat.

Is Phoebe pregnant?

I try to remember when the last time she mentioned having her period was. It *does* seem like a while ago, but I'm not exactly keeping track. But then I think about her moodiness, her sudden distance, and the pieces click into place.

Even more so once I root out the index card stuffed into the box. It's torn in half, but it's easy enough to piece back together and read. A list of reasons why having a baby with me would "never work."

Fuck.

I stare at the last item on the list. *Easton doesn't want me.* That could not be further from the truth. But if that's how Phoebe feels, then I clearly have been a terrible fake husband.

I need to talk to my wife.

I whip around to hurry from the room and nearly trip over Roger in my haste.

"Damn it," I tell him. "This is your fault, you know. She says I wouldn't take care of my own child? Doesn't she know I feed you every time you yowl at me?"

Roger meows reproachfully, unhelpful beast that he is. I ignore him, taking the stairs two at a time.

I'm not sure what I plan to do or how I can fix this. All I know is that I'm not letting my fake wife leave me over our very real baby. If Phoebe is pregnant, I'm going to make this work, any way I can.

CHAPTER 22

PHOEBE

"Seriously, I'm not being one of those 'hey I know two gay guys, I should get them together' type friends," I say, leaning against my spin bike as my instructor, Andre, putters around wiping down the handles of everyone's cycles. "I genuinely think you'd like him."

The gym has emptied out already, but I'm lingering.

Okay, half of me wants to avoid going home. I know Easton will be up and about by now, and I'm still not entirely sure how to feel about the negative pregnancy test. I mean, obviously it's one less complication to worry about. But I don't know why I feel so... *weird* about the result.

But the other half of me, the half that's been coming to this gym ever since I moved into Easton's place, honestly thinks this would be a good setup.

"No offense, but... how would I know that?" Andre

wipes sweat from his brow and fires me one of his sly little *I'm joking but not entirely* grins. Which is exactly why I want him to meet Monty, who's also always giving me those looks.

Then again, introducing these two could spell disaster for me. They both tease me enough separately as is.

"Fair," I admit. "It's just, your senses of humor seem really similar. And you both have that work-hard play-hard mentality…"

"Let me guess, he's a cross-fit instructor?" Andre fires me another smirk.

"Bartender."

"Oh, *God* no. Don't you know the first rule of New York City? Never date a bartender."

I snort. "Go back in time and tell that to my twenty-one-year-old self, please."

"You mean you're *not* twenty-one?" Andre gives me a lingering once-over, his gaze pausing for longer than strictly necessary on my backside. "That ass says otherwise."

Which makes me laugh and pop my hip for him, sticking out my ass. "You sure know how to win over the ladies."

"How do you think I got assigned this class time? It's the most popular slot. All the rich married women love me." Andre winks.

"I have a feeling their husbands don't share that sentiment," growls a voice from the doorway, startling us both.

I whip around to find Easton leaning against the glass door that leads out to the street, wearing a scowl so deep it shadows his eyes. *How long has he been standing there?* My heart does an awkward backflip.

But Easton isn't looking at me. He's glowering at Andre as though the poor man just came onto me.

Andre, for his part, can take a hint. He raises both hands in the universal *wasn't me* gesture and takes a sliding step backward in the direction of the changing rooms.

As for me, I fix my husband with a glare to rival his own. "Since when are you interested in spin classes?"

"Since I discovered my wife getting ogled by the instructor."

I roll my eyes. "Green is not a good color on you."

Easton pushes off the wall and steps toward me. I glance over my shoulder to doublecheck that Andre has disappeared into the men's changing area. It's just Easton and me. Well, us and all of New York City potentially watching us through the big ground floor windows of the studio. I peek through those and catch more than a few curious glances directed our way. Then, with another eyeroll, I grab Easton's elbow and yank him toward the changing rooms.

"Anyone in here?" I call, pushing open the door to the women's side, even though I know everyone from my class has cleared out already.

Easton hesitates in the doorway, but only for a split second. Then he follows my gaze, realizing the potential for an audience out in the main gym, and follows me into the room. He waits until the door swings shut behind me.

"If you're trying to make me jealous—" he starts, but I cut him off.

"I wasn't, but good to know it's this freaking easy." I cross my arms and glower at him. "Are you seriously going to become one of those husbands who stalk their wives and insist no other man comes within three feet of them?"

He stares right back. After a pause though, he looks at the floor and runs a hand through his hair. He lets out a slow breath. "Maybe I overreacted. But, look, Phoebe..." When he raises his eyes again, there's an expression in them I don't recognize. He looks... sincere. More than that. He almost seems desperate. "My emotions are all out of whack, but I'm sure that's nothing compared to what you're going through right now."

"What I'm... going through?" I repeat slowly.

He clears his throat once. Twice. Ducks his head again. "I found the box."

I raise an eyebrow. "If this is code for something—"

"The pregnancy test kit. I saw it, and your index cards." He pushes off the closed door and steps toward me.

Suddenly, I'm aware of how small these changing rooms are. How little space there is between our bodies. Is it just me, or is it getting hotter in here all of a sudden?

"Easton—"

"I want you to know I support you. Whatever you

want to do. It's completely up to you. But if you do want to keep it—"

I can't take this anymore. "I'm not pregnant," I blurt, which makes his mouth snap shut. Some of the intense heat fades from his eyes.

"Good," he replies without missing a beat.

And all at once, I feel like I'm being sucker-punched. I feel the same rush of weird, impossible-to-understand disappointment I felt when the pee stick stayed blank and white. *Negative.* I look away, anywhere but at Easton, because I can't stand to see his expression of relief. I can't stand to watch him feel good about the fact that he won't have to support me and a child, that he won't be tethered to me for any longer than he needs to be.

I understand, I really do. But I just... can't face him right now.

I brush past him to grab my gym bag, not even bothering to change out of my sweaty clothes. "Thanks for your support," I say, throwing the bag across my shoulder and striding back toward the door. "But I don't need or want it."

Easton blocks my path. He doesn't say anything. Not until I finally look up to meet his eyes.

"Yes," he says, his voice a low thrum that pulses all the way into my navel. "You do."

"Oh, because I belong to you now, is that it?" I square up to him, angrier than I've ever felt.

"No."

He's so close I can smell his shampoo, the pine-scented one I've watched him lather on during showers we've taken together. Just thinking about that is enough to make my stomach tighten, my heart beating so fast I feel it all throughout my body. My thighs tighten, and I can already tell I'm getting wet, in spite of myself.

Damn him. Damn my body for reacting to him. Damn everything about this situation.

But before I can extricate myself, he leans closer, his breath a searing heat against my cheek. "Because I'm your husband. And husbands support their wives."

It takes me by surprise, how intense my reaction to that feels. A rush of something like relief, mingled with utter disbelief. He's talking like we're actual partners. Like this is more than an arrangement, or a physical... whatever we've turned into.

"I..." My voice sticks in my throat.

It doesn't help that Easton takes advantage, sliding my bag off my shoulder. It hits the gym floor with a thud that echoes through the empty changing room. Then his hand returns to my shoulder, and his other cups my chin, turns my face to his. His eyes, when they meet mine, are filled with an intensity that mirrors how I'm feeling right now.

I'm still mad at him. Mad, and sad, and confused, and a million other emotions I can't even process. So when he leans in, it's almost a relief to let all that go. To drown it in a flood of desire instead.

I tilt my face to his and let him back me up against the wall, kissing me hard.

CHAPTER 23

EASTON

Everything I've felt since the moment I walked into the gym to the sight of my wife's spin instructor complimenting her ass—no, actually, since the moment I found the pregnancy test kit in my wife's desk—floods away. There's only Phoebe, and me, and my burning, desperate *need*.

I back her up against the wall, pinning her there as I dip to kiss her jawline, her collarbone.

"Easton," she whispers.

But I don't want to talk. I don't want to consider the crushing disappointment that shot through me when I learned Phoebe isn't pregnant. All I want is her. Now.

"You don't need support, hmm?" I grip her ass tightly and lift her body, pinning her to the wall until she wraps her legs around my waist to brace herself. "Are you sure about that?"

I push into her and kiss her again before she can respond, my tongue parting her lips to toy with hers. Her breath catches. Her scent wraps around me, and I taste a hint of salt on her lips from her workout. But it only makes me harder, because this is how she tastes after we've finished fucking. I can feel my cock pressed against her pussy in this position, feel the way she tenses when I cup one of her breasts through the fabric of her workout bra, making her gasp and arch into my palm.

Her nipple already feels hard, but it grows stiffer as I gently roll my thumb against it. Still kissing her, I shift to open my jeans. Phoebe lets her legs drop, and her hands slide down my chest, over my abs, tracing the edges through my shirt, until they rest over mine. She pushes my hands away and undoes my jeans for me.

"Who's supporting who now?" she asks, arching a brow, and there she is. The wife I married. All mouth.

"If we're keeping score..." I slide my hands over the soft arch of her waist, her hips, until I hook my thumbs beneath the waistband of her leggings. I peel them down slowly, exposing inch after inch of her soft, smooth skin.

Phoebe shivers as the cool air of the locker room hits her. But she doesn't stop her work either. She unzips my jeans and shoves them down my thighs and grips my cock through the fabric of my boxers, tracing my length with both palms. It draws a faint groan from the back of my throat, and her eyes, when they meet mine again, are hooded.

"How can I be so pissed and so thirsty for you at the same time?" she asks unexpectedly, and I have to grin.

"You have no idea how often I ask myself that question."

I slide her panties down as she pushes my boxers down, and I step forward. She responds by wrapping one leg around my waist, and I pull up her knee so the other can join it. I wrap my arms around her ass and my fingers find their way at once to her slit, like they've already memorized her whole body.

She's slick against my fingers, wet with want. I stroke her slowly, drawing it out. Savoring the hitch in her breath, the tremble in her shoulders, I pin her against the wall.

"You drive me crazy, you know that?" Phoebe murmurs.

With each stroke, I feel all the blood in my body rushing south, making me dizzy. Blind with desire. "Not nearly as crazy as you make me."

"Prove it," she breathes, and I don't need to be told twice.

I grip her ass in one hand, a soft, maddening handful, and press her shoulders to the tile with the other, my mouth hovering over hers. She tries to kiss me, but I shift, kissing the corner of her lips instead, the edge of her neck.

"I can't stand how much I need you," I say, barely thinking, barely aware of the words.

I position myself at her entrance, feel her hips press forward to angle herself, and when my cock finally pushes inside her, it feels like coming home and losing myself all at once.

I lose track of where we are. I forget why I came here, what upset me, why I was angry. All I can think about is Phoebe's hands tracing over my back, burying in my hair. Her mouth, hard and hot against mine. Her body pressed against me so tightly I feel every inch of her soft curves. Her pussy clenching around my cock as I pull back and drive into her, again and again.

It feels so good, I forget we've done this before.

At least, until she comes with a cry that echoes throughout the changing room. I finish a few minutes later, driving into her with one final thrust as I come. Then I step back, both of us red-faced and breathless, and watch the realization hit her at the same time it does me.

"Was that..." She pauses. Tries to catch her breath.

"A repeat?" I finish for her.

It was. We fucked against a wall our very first night together, in fact. The expression on Phoebe's face is unreadable. Relief? Anger?

The emotions I've been trying to avoid come flooding back. The pregnancy test. My own jealousy—over what? This fake relationship?

I recall her words the night we made this bargain. *We'll be through the whole repertoire... then this buzz will fade and we'll get over each other.* I turn away so she can't see my expression. Can't see how much it's killing me to think about that.

"Well, guess we're that boring married couple already. Didn't even take a year." I try to keep my tone lighthearted, joking.

When I look back, Phoebe is pulling on her clothes, grabbing her bag. Her hair came loose as we fucked, and it covers her face now, wild and messy.

"Guess so," she replies, her voice thick with derision. "It was fun while it lasted." With that, she brushes past me, out of the changing room.

I stare at the door as it swings shut, feeling like absolute hell.

CHAPTER 24

PHOEBE

Easton is avoiding me. Either that, or work is conveniently super busy right after our fight. Fuck? Fuck up? I don't even know what it was. I don't get what *any* of this has become.

Why does my fake marriage suddenly involve so much real heartache?

For the next three days, I search for the answer in the bottom of several tubs of Ben & Jerry's while holed up in the movie room at the house. But even my usual go-to, *10 Things I Hate About You*, isn't enough to pull me out of this funk. My index cards lay scattered around me like wounded animals. Every now and then I halfheartedly work on my thesis outlines, but those soon join the index cards on the floor as I queue up another romcom.

By the time I work my way into the Nicholas Sparks-style tragi-romcoms, I'm feeling just plain pathetic.

What was I expecting? I knew I shouldn't have mixed business with pleasure. Introducing sex into a formal arrangement was a surefire way to heartbreak. All it took was one pregnancy scare before my husband decided to repeat positions, knowing it would be our last hookup.

I'm starting on a new tub of Chocolate Fudge Brownie and *The Notebook* when the intercom buzzes. I ignore it, assuming it's a delivery person or someone selling door-to-door Jesus, and honestly, Easton pays the doorman to deal with all of that. But a minute later, it buzzes again, longer and more insistently.

I frown and check the time on my phone. Eleven o'clock on a Wednesday morning. Who would be visiting at this hour? Easton's obviously at work, and Monty doesn't wake up before one o'clock in the afternoon—the perils of bartender life.

While I'm considering the potentials, the buzzer rings again, for so long this time I hear a thunder on the staircase and spot Roger's tail whipping into my bedroom.

He hates that buzzer. Poor guy.

Groaning, I lever myself off the couch and pull on a sweater. I'm dressed haphazardly in sweats, my hair a wild mess because I didn't bother to shower today. Why would I? Nobody but Ryan Gosling and Rachel McAdams were going to see me today. And Roger, of course. But Roger has seen me at my worst and still loves me anyway.

Unlike some people.

Before I can reach the intercom to connect to the

doorman, there's a knock at the door. I yell, "Hold on a second, Christ," as I yank it open. Only for my jaw to drop.

Standing on our doorstep, dressed so sharply it would make Meryl Streep flinch, is Easton's grandmother.

"Sofia. Hi."

Over the last few months, I've seen her at a couple of family dinners, and one work event Easton dragged me to that involved the world's most awkward team-building exercise: group bowling. But this is the first time I've been alone with her in... well. Ever.

Sofia sizes me up, her nose wrinkling ever so slightly. "I see you're not in much better shape." Then she brushes past me into the house.

"Oh, um... Easton's not here," I say, then realize I'm not one hundred percent sure about that. The only signs of life I've seen from him in three days are a bedroom light turning on when he returns late at night. Presumably from work. Or maybe from finding some new, non-boring girl to fuck, I don't know.

"I know that." Grandma Sofia fixes me with her most imperious stare. "He's at the office. Where he has been all but sleeping for the last three days." She drags a stool out from the kitchen counter and perches on it, looking for all the world like an interviewer. Or a police inter-rogator. "What happened?"

I blink. Lick my lips once, twice. "What makes you think something happened?" I can't bring myself to meet her steely glare.

Sofia snorts. "I wasn't born yesterday. I recognize marital trouble when I see it." She waves at me.

I would be offended, except that when I glance down, I notice more than one ice cream stain on my threadbare pajama bottoms. I swallow a groan. "It doesn't matter."

"Why, because your marriage is a sham?" She arches a brow, and that stops me in my tracks.

I freeze, my gaze darting around the apartment, like I might be able to spot an escape-hatch somewhere. *Fuck.* This is the *one* person we're meant to be fooling. The whole reason Easton dragged me into this mess. And now here she is, springing an interrogation on me at the worst possible moment.

"I—"

"Don't bother denying it," Grandma Sofia cuts in. "I've suspected from the beginning. Although I didn't confirm it until last night. Easton left your *contract* lying on his desk. He must really be out of sorts to get so careless."

She says *contract* the way someone else might say *cockroach*. It does nothing to help my already frayed nerves.

"It's not a sham," I say, because I know Easton would want me to deny it. Yet the words emerge with more feeling than I expected to be able to muster. My stomach sinks. Because I realize that's true. For me, at least. "I mean, maybe it started out that way, but now I..." *Oh, God.* "I think I love him," I murmur, more to myself than Sofia.

She watches me as if we're talking about nothing

more complicated than the weather. "You *think* you love your husband? How terribly old-fashioned."

I shake my head. "Except he doesn't... I mean. I don't know how he feels. We—I... thought I was pregnant. And it made me realize I want kids. But Easton doesn't, and now everything is a mess." When I look up again, I can practically feel the desperation rolling off me in waves.

Grandma Sofia sighs. For the first time since barging in here, she looks genuinely sympathetic. She pats my hand where it rests on the kitchen counter. "My grandson can be an idiot sometimes." That startles a weak laugh out of me. "Which is a shame, because I liked you."

Liked. Past tense already. I shut my eyes to try to stem a sudden and horrifyingly embarrassing rush of tears. "Right. Message received."

"What message?" Grandma Sofia levers herself back upright. "I just came here to verify things with you before I confront my grandson."

Great. Now on top of everything else, I've completely blown our cover. If Easton doesn't already hate me and want me out of his life, he will now.

I blink away more tears as Sofia pats my shoulder. "Don't feel guilty, dear. It's his mistake. These sort of things never pan out the way men expect them to."

A lump forms in my throat. All I manage is a weak nod. I don't even say goodbye as Sofia strides back across the open plan room, heels clicking, and lets herself out.

Only after she's gone do I raise my head to survey the house through watery eyes.

As much as it hurts, Sofia's right. These things never pan out. No one makes a fake marriage suddenly real. I glance at the ring on my finger. Part of my payment. But I failed at my job, so... I wriggle it off my finger and set it on the kitchen counter, where Easton will see it. Hopefully he'll be able to recoup the money he spent by pawning it.

As for the rest, the tuition money and the payments... I'll tell him to cancel it all. I don't feel right accepting it when our whole plan just came crashing down. I write him a short, curt note to that effect, then I beeline upstairs where I stowed my suitcases, already reaching for my phone.

I hope Monty's all right with me crashing on his couch until I find another place. Maybe he'll be able to get me my job at the Loft back too, although that seems like too much to hope for.

God, I'll miss free time. And this apartment.

But most of all... I'm going to miss my husband.

CHAPTER 25

EASTON

I don't realize I've fallen asleep on my desk until someone jabs me in the shoulder, hard. I startle upright, a page of something stuck to my cheek, and whip around to find Martin, my grandmother's secretary, standing beside me as straight-backed as a soldier at attention.

"Mrs. Taylor would like to see you in her office," Martin says. The man always speaks in an utter deadpan, but I could swear that this time, I see a faintly amused smile playing at the corners of his mouth before he bows and ducks away.

Groaning, I turn to shuffle all the paperwork on my desk together. Stacks upon stacks of projections and statements that I was sorting through, mainly to give myself a mind-numbing task that would keep my mind off of what an utter mess my personal life has become.

I realize I'm being a coward, hiding out here at the

office. But after Phoebe stormed out on me at the gym, with an "It was fun while it lasted," I haven't been able to bring myself to face her.

I can't stand the thought of seeing that derision on her face again. Or worse, what if I tell her how I've been feeling and she *pities* me?

After all, we were clear about the boundaries of this situation. And yes, okay, we redrew those boundaries a bit when we decided to make our fake marriage physical. But even then, we made clear rules about how long it would last. Only until we repeated ourselves.

I just didn't expect that to happen so quickly.

I didn't expect *any* of this to happen so quickly. Just over four months ago, I was single, oblivious to the fact that Phoebe Jones existed, and I was perfectly happy in every way.

Were you though? asks a part of my brain I don't normally acknowledge.

Life was simpler, maybe. There was no cat leaving tufts of fur all over my sofa, and no woman leaving piles of study material everywhere either. I could hook up with anyone I wanted. But if I'm honest, none of my hookup sex could hold a candle to sex with Phoebe. And as frustrating as her messiness can sometimes be, it makes my apartment feel less like a museum and more like home.

Hell, I've even started to get along with the damn cat.

I run my hands through my hair and try to straighten myself up as best I can for whatever my grandmother wants. I finish scooping the paperwork into my top desk drawer and freeze.

There, at the bottom of the stack of tax files for this quarter, sits an all-too-familiar folder. The file my lawyer gave me—my copy of the contract Phoebe and I drew up. A vague, fuzzy memory comes back to me. Last night, my brain fritzing from three days of barely any sleep, I dragged this contract out to reread it, as if it might hold the answer to how I can get myself out of this bind.

And then...

I put it away again, didn't I? Locked it back in the drawer where I've kept it safely hidden from prying eyes?

I can't remember.

"Fuck," I hiss.

I drop the folder into my drawer and lock the whole desk. Nobody saw. It was buried in other papers. Right? I grab my coffee cup and drain it, wincing over how stale and cold it is. Then I lever myself upright and straighten my wrinkled suit jacket. Either way, I can't leave my grandmother waiting for too long. She doesn't like that.

With a deep breath and a prayer to whatever deity might be listening, I cross the floor to my grandmother's corner office. The door is cracked, but I knock anyway.

"Enter," she says, and from that one word, I can tell I am in deep shit.

I step into her office and ease the door shut. Grandma Sofia doesn't stand to greet me. She fixes me with a glare that has haunted my nightmares since childhood, gesturing at the spare seat across from her.

I sink into it, aware of how much smaller it is than

her desk chair. Despite the many, many inches I have on her, in this chair, I'm forced to look up at her glowering expression. I swear she set her office up this way on purpose.

"Is there something you need?" I ask, when the silence between us stretches thin.

She purses her lips. "Yes. I need my grandson to be honest with me."

I resist the urge to squirm. "I'm always honest with you, Grandma."

"Are you?" She arches a brow. "Because I just came back from your apartment, where I had an *extremely* enlightening conversation with your wife. Or should I call her your employee?"

Fuck, fuck, fuck. "It's not what you think."

"You mean you didn't hire a virtual stranger to pretend to be your wife in order to trick me into thinking you were mature enough to take over my seat on this company's board?" She folds her hands on the desk and smiles. That smile isn't comforting. It screams *danger*.

"Okay, maybe it's a *little bit* what you think, but—"

"Do you think I'm stupid, Easton?"

I blink, taken aback. "Of course not. You're the smartest person I know."

She rolls her eyes. "Flattery won't save you."

"I mean it, Grandma. I look up to you. I always have; you know that."

"And yet, you went out of your way to conduct this whole charade. Why? Are you that eager to get rid of me? To sentence me to the obscurity of retirement? Or do you want to advance your own career that badly that you don't mind throwing your family under the bus to get ahead?"

"No! No, it's nothing like that." I breathe out hard through my nose. "It's... look, Grandma, you built this company up from nothing. You still feel attached—and I completely understand that. But, lately... some of the deals we've been making haven't exactly been forward-looking. We haven't been acting in the company's best interest."

"By *we* you mean *me*?" She narrows her eyes.

I square my shoulders. "Yes. And I'm not the only board member who feels this way." I hold up a hand to stave off any more questions. "I don't want to hurt you, I swear. And if it was just about my career, I wouldn't care. But I know how much you care about this company, and I don't want to see your dreams damaged because..."

"Because an old woman doesn't know when to let go," Grandma Sofia finishes, when the words fail me. She leans back in her seat for the first time since I walked into the office and stares at her folded hands. "You could have simply told me this, you realize."

"I'm pretty sure I did."

"I'm pretty sure you danced around the subject instead of engaging me in a straightforward, if awkward, conversation."

"Can you blame me?"

"I can blame you for choosing an elaborate ruse instead." She lifts both eyebrows this time.

I rub the back of my neck. "I just knew how important it was to you that I settle down. I thought it would ease the sting, maybe."

"And how did all that lying work out for you, grandson?" She glances down pointedly, and I follow her gaze, taking in the wrinkles on my shirt sleeves where I dozed off with my head pillowed on my arms.

My sigh turns into a groan. "Not great. Turns out if you fake it hard enough, it can get real."

Sofia blinks. For the first time since I walked in here, she looks surprised. "Are you saying…?"

I tip my head back to stare at the ceiling. Anything to avoid her terrifying eye contact. "I think I'm in love with my wife."

"How terribly old-fashioned of you," she drawls. When I look back at her again, she's actually smiling.

"Are you enjoying this?" I grumble.

"A little. It does seem a tad karmic." She waves. "All right, so you love her. What are you going to do about it?"

"We agreed this would just be a professional thing, so… I guess I have to terminate our contract." My insides quail just thinking about it.

No more Phoebe meeting me at the door in lingerie. No more Phoebe flashing index cards with some new question scrawled on it, waiting for me to give her my answer or to guess hers. No more Phoebe cuddled up beside me in bed, watching dawn paint our curtains with light.

"Ah yes, because that's the only possible solution to loving someone. Dump them." Now it's my grandmother's turn to roll her eyes. I definitely inherited my abilities from her.

"Well, when you put it like *that*," I say, sarcasm lacing my tone.

But she's right. I should at least tell Phoebe how I really feel. Even if it makes her run for the hills even faster than she must already want to. She deserves to know.

Across the desk, my grandmother's glare softens. "Anyone can put a ring on it, Easton. For, as you've now learned, any number of inane reasons. But do you know what makes a marriage real? Honesty. Both with your partner *and* with yourself."

Honesty. Weirdly, for all our marriage's fake origins, I have been honest with Phoebe about so many things. All those flash cards come back to me now. The personal stories we've shared. I can't remember the last time I shared so much with someone I dated. Maybe I never have.

And that alone makes me realize what I need to do.

I stand up all at once. "I've got to go."

Grandma Sofia barely contains a smirk. "I assumed as much."

But on the threshold of her office, I glance back at her, frowning. "Actually though, before I do. Have you got any spare index cards?"

CHAPTER 26

PHOEBE

It takes longer than I expected to pack. A lot longer than it took me to pack to leave my old apartment, which seems weird, because I lived there for years and I've only been living at Easton's for just over four months.

Has it really been that long?

Somehow, it feels like forever and the blink of an eye at the same time.

But after a couple of hours, I manage to locate all the stuff I'd scattered to the far reaches of his giant condo. My lingerie comes down from Easton's dresser upstairs, along with some cat toys I found under his bed and a bag of cat treats hidden in the nightstand.

Wait a minute. Was Easton sneaking Roger treats? I stare at the half-empty bag, unable to remember if I bought this one or not.

It would explain why Roger's looking a little chunkier around the hips...

Shaking my head, I pack the treats, and head downstairs to scrounge up all the stray study supplies and clothes I've left in the living room, kitchen, study, and even some notecards on the staircase.

Damn. Maybe I really should try to be a bit tidier in my next apartment.

My next apartment without Easton. I push the thought aside.

Monty told me I could crash on his couch for a couple of weeks, so at least for the time being, I have somewhere to go. And he's going to ask at the Murray Loft tonight if there are any server openings. I should be focused on that, or on how I'll job hunt if that gig isn't a possibility.

But all I can think about, as I drift through the house doing one last sweep for any stray possessions I forgot, is Easton. It's like all the memories we shared here have become ghosts stalking me. I remember him cooking breakfast for me one lazy Sunday. Forcing him to watch *Sleepless in Seattle* for the first time, curled up together in the movie room. Him helping me study, quizzing me with flash cards as we sprawled across the living room couch.

And then us forgetting all about the flash cards and getting lost in each other instead, our hands sliding beneath one another's shirts, our tongues finding new places to trail across each other's bodies.

A lump forms in the back of my throat. It refuses to go away, no matter how many times I swallow.

"It's for the best," I tell myself as I zip up my suitcase, then lug it downstairs into the foyer. "If this went on any longer, you'd be even *more* attached, Phoebe." At least, that's what I try to tell myself.

All the while, the ring winks at me from the kitchen counter, accusatory.

Part of me knows I ought to be practical. Keep that at least, even if I refuse everything else Easton planned to pay me. It would crush my student loans. But I can't bring myself to do it. Taking the ring feels wrong when I'm the one walking out.

Taking the ring would make it feel as though this whole thing really *was* fake. And it's not, I finally realize.

Not to me.

I leave Roger until last, which is probably a mistake. As soon as he sees me touch the cat carrier, he goes running and darts underneath the living room sofa, to the farthest corner where he knows I can't reach him.

Groaning, I flatten myself on the carpet and strain with one arm, trying to grab his scruff. "Come *on*, Roger. We've worn out our welcome here, okay?"

He glares at me.

I glare right back. "You're the one who was all grumpy and hissy the day we moved in. Don't you want to get away from mean old grumpy Easton?"

I've almost got him. I press my whole shoulder under the couch and manage to touch Roger's paw. He claws my hand and bolts away before I can react, speeding past my face and galloping upstairs.

"You brat!" I yell after him. "It's not *my* fault your stepfather hates you!"

"Who said I hate him?"

Easton's voice makes me freeze halfway up the staircase, midway through chasing my cat. I turn slowly and find him poised in the doorframe. I didn't even hear him come in, I was so distracted by Roger. My heart does the strangest backflip, part hope and part *pain*, because... shit.

Easton looks almost as terrible as I've been feeling.

His eyes are puffy, spidered with red, and there are purple bags underneath. His hair is even more rumpled than usual, and there are actual wrinkles in his normally pressed-to-perfection suit. Until this very moment, I didn't realize it was possible for clothing to wrinkle in Easton's presence. I thought he'd simply glare at it until it straightened itself out.

Easton glances at the kitchen counter and freezes. I know what he's seeing. He crosses to the ring, and I want to curl into a ball right here and die.

This isn't how I imagined this going. I didn't think I'd have to face him before I left. I thought I could slink out and away and not have to deal with all the emotions building up inside me.

Instead, I'm forced to watch Easton pocket the ring and I feel like I'm dying. But then my brain, which had short-circuited at his sudden appearance, finally reboots. I think about what he said when he walked in and wonder if my ears are broken. "You... don't hate Roger?"

Easton turns to face me again. He steps closer, and I

find myself doing the same without meaning to, my feet drifting slowly down the stairs until I meet him at the bottom.

"No." Easton holds my gaze. This close, even with all his rumpledness, there's still something piercing about him, impossible to look away from. "In fact, it's hard to imagine living without him. I don't want to."

Somehow I have a feeling we're not talking about the cat anymore. But I raise my chin anyway. "Well, you're not keeping him in the divorce. Wasn't that in the prenup? I could've sworn I put in a clause—"

"I don't want a divorce," Easton says.

My ears really must be broken. I glance at his pocket, where his hand has formed a fist around what I assume is the ring I just gave back. He follows my gaze, and I notice the muscles around his jaw tighten, a shadow coming into his eyes.

"Look, I know I'm leaving a bit earlier than planned," I babble. "But to be honest, things have gotten, um, complicated, and—"

I stop talking, because Easton has pulled something from his pocket. Not the ring after all. A stack of... flash cards?

He holds up the first one. It's yellow. One of Easton's answers then. On the front, in his now-familiar handwriting, he's scrawled DEALS WITH COMPLEX EMOTIONS BY:

I arch an eyebrow. He just stares back at me, dead serious.

"I don't know, also eating ice cream?" I guess.

He flips the card around. *Running away. Or being an ass.*

I can't help it. I laugh. "Okay, another one we have in common." I step closer to him. "Sometimes running away is just easier."

We're so close now I catch the scent of his familiar shampoo and the aftershave brand he keeps at the office.

"Trust me, I know." He smiles, but it looks more self-deprecating than anything. Then he tosses that card aside. There's another one behind it.

SIGNS HE'S FALLING IN LOVE WITH YOU:

"Easton." I search his face. His eyes.

He's gazing back at me so fixedly, I couldn't tear myself away if I wanted to. And I don't.

"Not going to lie, this is a hard one to guess," he says softly. "I didn't even recognize it myself, for a long time. What with this being the first time I ever have and all..."

I bite my lower lip. Suddenly, the room swims around me. But I blink, and it rights itself, and I realize, nope. Those are just tears. I always thought happy tears were the sort of dramatic thing that only happened in movies, but—

"Are you saying...?"

He turns the card around. *1. He no longer hates your cat.*

I stifle a ridiculous, enormous smile. "That's it?"

"Okay, so I couldn't fit all my answers on one card this time." He drops it. Behind it is another index card, only the answer this time. *2. He actually likes the house more when you leave it a little messy (keyword: a LITTLE).*

Now I'm full-on laughing. And probably blushing. "If this is your attempt at *Love Actually*-ing me, it's working."

"Never seen it, but good to know."

"Oh my *God,* we have to—" I break off as he drops this card too.

3. He can't stop thinking about you. That card flutters to the floor. *4. He actually wants to repeat sexual positions. Many of them. Many, many times.*

I shake my head and press one hand to my mouth. I'm not sure if I'm holding back a smile or something more embarrassing. My stomach keeps doing backflips as though I'm on a ride at Coney Island, and my head swims.

5. But most of all, there's something else he wants to repeat.

I'm still standing there like a complete weirdo, hand clamped over my mouth, when Easton sinks to one knee. This time, he does take the ring back out of his pocket. Along with one last flash card. This one, unlike the rest, is red. One that I'm meant to answer.

WILL YOU MARRY ME?

"But—" I squeak around the palm still pressed to my face, and he holds up an index finger.

"For real this time, Phoebe." He looks so nervous and hopeful and desperate at once that my heart feels like it's trying to swell straight out of my chest. "I realize I... this isn't fake for me anymore. I love you."

Now my eyes are seriously watering. I shut them, but that means I can't look at Easton, so I open them again almost immediately, ignoring the tear that creeps down my cheek. Then I sink to my knees beside him. "Yes. *Yes, Easton, I love you t—*"

The rest of my words get swallowed up when he kisses me. We break apart just long enough for him to study my eyes again, like he's checking for take-backs. "Are you sure? Because—"

I swat his arm. "Don't you know me at all by now? I wouldn't say it if I wasn't sure." I cup his face and gaze into those dark eyes. "I love you, Easton Taylor."

"Taylor-Jones now, I think." He winks.

Then he kisses me again, harder, and I let him tip me backward onto the index cards strewn about the hallway floor.

And neither of us even care, when we tear off one another's clothes, that this is a repeat.

CHAPTER 27

EASTON

For once, my grandmother's completely overbearing nature is working in my favor. At first, when she demanded a whole new wedding ceremony—"since your initial vows were made under the guise of deception, they're null and void in my book"—I was worried Phoebe wouldn't be into it, or that the whole wedding planning nightmare would drive her to beg for an elopement to Hawaii.

But if anything, the many late nights discussing seating charts and invitation lists and whether it was ethical to have flowers (we compromised on seasonal flowers from a local florist—the greenest option apparently), only strengthened us.

We wound up making a whole lot of new flash cards about each of our usual argument techniques, at least.

I still maintain that I'm right about taking Roger off

the guest list. Phoebe only conceded after she tried packing him into a carrier for a test run, to see if she could carry him to the church for the ceremony, and he yowled so loudly I'm sure passersby on the street thought we were murdering him.

But all the late nights and plans and arguments were worth it for this moment. Standing beside the altar, watching Phoebe walk up the aisle, her mother on one arm and her father on the other, I've never felt anything like this rush of happiness, excitement, and sheer fucking shock at my dumb luck.

I never imagined I'd get married. But then, I never imagined dating a woman like Phoebe either. Hell, I didn't even know women like her existed until I talked her into being my partner-in-con.

She catches me staring and winks, before turning to hug each of her parents in turn.

This gown fits her a lot better than the one she wore at our first wedding. But I'd marry her in a burlap sack if it was what she wanted.

She climbs the steps to join me at the altar, and I catch her hands at the top, running my thumbs over the backs. It takes everything in me not to kiss her right here and now—my grandmother insisted we uphold that whole "no seeing the bride for the whole day before the ceremony" tradition, which means I haven't kissed her since we parted last night, each to separate rooms in the full hotel my grandmother insisted on reserving for this.

Over Phoebe's shoulder, her man of honor, Monty, flashes me a surreptitious thumbs-up. Beside him stand

Phoebe's bridesmaids, and at the end of the row, my sister, Sydney, rolls her eyes. But beneath her usual snark, I can tell she's enjoying this too.

Phoebe glances over my shoulder, and I'm sure Max and Dylan are giving her similar encouraging nods. That, or making rude gestures behind my back. But I'm pretty sure even they wouldn't do that with my grandmother watching from the front row of the ballroom, eagle-eyed as ever.

The place is packed. My grandmother insisted on inviting half the company, plus the whole extended family, friends of the family, what seems like everyone I ever went to college with... But as the minister calls for silence, they all fade away.

For me, there's only Phoebe. Her hands in mine, her eyes fixed on me.

This time, when the minister has us repeat after him, neither of our voices waver. "I, Easton Taylor, do take this woman, to have and to hold..."

And this time, when he says, "You may now kiss the bride," it's no light kiss between strangers.

I cup Phoebe's head in one hand, my fingers tangling in the curls she did for the occasion. I bend down in slow motion, feel every second of her eyes on me, her mouth parting in anticipation. When my lips touch hers, it's a slow, deep kiss. And when I bend her backward, my other arm cradling her waist, she moves with me, with the complete trust that comes from two people who know each other better than anyone else.

By the time we're standing again, the applause has

reached thunderous levels. I catch a few whoops and catcalls in there, mainly from Dylan and Max. But I don't turn to look. I just stare straight into Phoebe's eyes, grinning. And she grins right back.

"What do you think, better this time?" I arch a brow.

"I'd say we're improving." She rests a hand against my chest as I draw her back to her feet. Then she tilts her head and considers the dress and the ring on her finger. "But I dunno. Maybe we'll have to get married again in a few years just to make sure. Third time's the charm?"

I snort. "Admit it, you just want an excuse to buy more dresses."

"Honestly, I thought I was happy living in sweatpants and T-shirts, but now that I've had a taste of the princess life—"

I cut her off by kissing her again, then we're descending the steps to process out of the ballroom, a train of guests following in our wake. I spot Dylan with his date-of-the-week, and Max trading barbs with Sydney.

Before I can think too hard about it though, we reach the reception area of the hotel, and the greeting of the guests begins in earnest. Starting with Grandma Sofia, who corners us before we've even reached the spot where we're meant to stand and greet the rest of our families and friends.

"There now, wasn't that much better than a courthouse?" She offers her cheek, and I bend to kiss it.

"You were right, Grandma."

Her eyes practically sparkle. "Come again? I didn't quite catch that..."

Phoebe laughs and holds out her arms, and Sofia pulls her into a hug.

"Thank you," Phoebe says. "If it weren't for Easton being so worried about what you think, we never would have met."

My grandmother laughs. "Thank *you,* my dear. I don't know that any other woman could have wrangled my grandson quite so effectively."

I roll my eyes. "I'm not *that* hard to deal with."

Now both of them laugh, which makes me shoot my wife a glare. *My wife.*

But my grandmother is too distracted to notice. She's patting her pockets, then withdrawing a slim envelope. "Your gift."

"You don't have to—"

"Open it."

I glance behind Sofia. A line stretches out the door and back into the ballroom, people waiting to greet us. But my grandmother is nothing if not undeterrable. Sighing, I slit open the envelope and peer inside. There's nothing except a folded slip of paper. I frown, confused, and withdraw it.

Notice of resignation.

I glance from the slip to my grandmother and back, my eyes widening. "You—"

"I stepped down yesterday." My grandmother smiles. "You were right. It's time. It's been time for a while." She pats my shoulder. "I hear the board plans to meet next week to confirm it, but allow me to pre-congratulate you." She winks.

Phoebe grins so wide that I get the feeling she was in on this too. She squeezes my shoulder. "You deserve it, hubby."

"But don't you dare let him work on the honeymoon," Grandma Sofia adds, shaking a finger first at Phoebe, then at me, before she departs.

"I have *some* work-life balance," I protest, but I'm only talking to empty air.

Phoebe just snorts.

Then the next guest steps into Grandma's place, and we fall into newlywed host mode. At least this part passes relatively quickly, since everyone is eager for the night ahead—drinks and dancing and food we spent weeks picking out. Somewhere up in my bedroom at home is an index card that says BEST PART OF WEDDING PLANNING, with *food and cake tasting* on the back.

But if I were to go back and write a BEST PART OF THE WEDDING ITSELF card, the only answer I could give would be *Phoebe*.

CHAPTER 28

PHOEBE

I readjust the mask over my eyes and groan. My pulse throbs against my temples. "Whose idea was it to leave the morning after the wedding again?"

"Pretty sure that was your call, darling wife."

I bury my face in Easton's shoulder. "Liar."

But my voice comes out muffled by his T-shirt—my wedding present to him. Matching brightly patterned casual T-shirts and sweatpants that I'm still shocked I managed to convince Easton Taylor to wear in public. He runs his hands through my hair, and it eases the headache a little.

The worst part is, I don't even think this is a hangover. Between all the guests we had to greet, extended family we both had to dance with, and what felt like a billion photos we had to pose for, I barely had two glasses of champagne, and both of those only during the toasts.

But between dancing all night in my enormous, gorgeous, and very hot gown, then Easton carrying me up into the vast honeymoon suite in the wee hours—a suite complete with a jacuzzi tub and the largest bed I've ever seen outside of the one in Easton's condo...

Well. Let's just say I did not get very much post-wedding sleep.

Then this morning was the ungodly early farewell brunch, before Norm sped us to the airport just in time to make our flight.

Monty's forgiven me for ditching our Hawaii plans to go early with Easton. But only because when he couldn't find a date for the wedding, I paired him with my spin instructor, Andre. And judging by the way the two of them disappeared before we'd even cut the cake, I have a feeling it went well. Plus, since Monty is cat-sitting Roger while we're away, Easton gave him the keys and free rein of the townhouse.

If Easton thinks *I'm* messy, he has no idea what he just signed up for. But hey, with your new bride comes her besties. He'll learn to deal.

The plane lurches into motion, and I groan again.

Easton keeps massaging my arm and bends down to kiss the top of my head. "We'll be in the air soon. Trust me, the lie-flat beds up here make all the difference."

I peek out from under my mask to survey the first-class seats again. I've never flown anything but economy. Gotta admit, this is a whole different world. I stretch my legs all the way out, and they *still* don't touch the seat in front of me. I wriggle my toes. "I can see how they would."

Then I notice the little gift box at my elbow. In Tiffany blue. I squint from it at Easton and back again.

"Okay, I know first class is fancy, but I'm pretty sure they don't give out free jewelry."

He laughs and nudges me. "Open it."

I squint at him, still suspicious, and flip open the lid. Inside, nestled on a blue velvet cushion, is a gold cat-shaped tag with curling font. *Roger Taylor-Jones.*

I let out a gasp that turns into a squeal. "You bought Roger a wedding present?"

"What kind of stepfather would I be if I neglected our son?" Easton's eyes sparkle.

I lean in to kiss him just as the plane lurches into the sky, throwing us together harder. I don't mind.

When we break apart, I meet his gaze, my grin so wide it almost hurts. "I have never been more attracted to you."

He laughs again, longer this time. "Damn, if I'd known it was this easy to win you over, I would've started spoiling your pussy a lot sooner."

"For the millionth time, stop calling him my pussy in public," I protest, but Easton cups my jaw, his eyes alight with mischief.

"Who said I was talking about Roger?" Then he's leaning in and I tilt forward, sinking into my husband's kiss.

By the time we break apart again, both of us are

breathing faster. He rests his forehead against mine and gazes into my eyes, arching one brow slowly.

"You know," he murmurs softly, "I can think of one position we haven't checked off our repertoire yet…"

"Does the mile high club count as a position or just a location?" I muse, before letting out a squeal as Easton pulls me back into his arms.

Either way, I have a feeling that no matter how many repeats we wind up having, marital sex will be anything but boring.

EPILOGUE

PHOEBE

I sprawl across the couch cushions, struggling to find a position that doesn't make my lower back ache. These days, everything makes my lower back ache.

"How is it possible that only a year ago, we were lying on a beach sipping mai tais from coconuts and I was wearing the world's skimpiest bikini?" I grumble.

"You could still fit into the bikini," Easton points out helpfully. "You just have company now." With that, he kisses my stomach through the fabric of my new maternity T-shirt.

Which, at this size, really feels more like wearing a small tent. Or a dress.

"I'm about ready for *the company* to vacate its current position already." I sigh and sink my head back against the headrest. My eight-and-a-half-month belly rises up beneath me like a foreign landscape.

But when Easton nudges my shirt higher and kisses my belly again, slower this time, working his tongue across the expanse in slow, careful circles... then I guess I don't mind it so much. Not entirely.

He traces his hands up my sides to cup my chest, and his tongue follows after. "Mm. Have I mentioned how sexy you look lately, wife?"

I swat his shoulder. "Not funny."

"I'm not joking." His eyes catch mine, and he *does* look serious.

There's a lot I didn't anticipate about pregnancy. The size, the body issues, the back pain. But I also didn't anticipate how sexy Easton can still make me feel with one simple word, a glance, a touch.

I smile at him. "Nice try, but we still have a test to prepare for."

Now it's his turn to groan. "Didn't you get your fill of tests and finals already?"

He goes back to pushing my shirt up and aside, then circling his tongue around my nipple, before gently catching it between his teeth. I sigh, my head falling back again.

Thankfully, I graduated months ago. With full honors, I might add, in spite of dealing with morning sickness and pregnancy brain throughout the last couple months that I was working on my thesis. Actually, if anything, I think being pregnant and thinking constantly about this baby's upcoming arrival to the world and how I would prepare him or her for life made me even more aware of how important clinical social work is. It shaped much of my thesis too.

But that doesn't mean my work is done. If anything, graduation was only the beginning.

Ignoring Easton as he does his best to maneuver my shirt off of me, I grab the stack of cards I worked on last night. "Okay, let's see…" I flip through until one catches my eye. "Ooh, here we go." I hold it up.

HOW OFTEN DO NEWBORNS EAT?

Easton looks up from my chest, eyebrows quirked. "Seriously?"

"This is important!"

"So is this!" He flicks my nipple with his tongue, and I squirm, rolling my eyes.

"Stop trying to distract me. It's time for your lesson, Mr. Taylor-Jones."

"Hmm." He sits back and studies me. "What do I receive if I get one right?"

I stifle a smile. "You want to make this interesting? Okay. Right answer, I lose a piece of clothing. Wrong answer, you do."

He grins. "Deal." Then he glances at the card. "Every two to three hours, by the way."

"That one doesn't count, you had time to think about it."

But Easton clicks his tongue. "Clothing off, Mrs. Taylor-Jones."

Suppressing a smirk, I wriggle the rest of the way out of my T-shirt and toss it aside. "Next card." I hold it out.

BEST NAME FOR A BOY.

Easton narrows his eyes. "Pretty sure this one is a matter of opinion."

"Oh, no, it's not," I reply. "There is most definitely a correct answer. And a wrong one."

"We are not naming the baby Roger," he grumbles.

I swat him with the index card. "I wouldn't do that to Roger! He's going to be jealous enough as it is."

Easton snorts. "Okay... Henry?"

"Oh, my *God*. Lose the shirt." I lean back, glaring at him.

"What's wrong with Henry?" he protests.

But he does grab the hem of his shirt and yank it over his head, so I suppose I can't complain too hard. Especially when he leans down along my length, his abs brushing over my prone form.

"It's an old man name. Do you want this baby to be a premature old man?"

"What if she's a girl?" Easton cocks his head.

"Oh, there's a card for that too." I smirk before letting Easton kiss me, long and slow, his tongue parting my lips.

"Should I guess that one next?" he murmurs, mouth still pressed to mine, before he kisses the corner of my lips, then along my jawline.

"Nooo, first you still have to figure out the right answer to this one."

Or at least, that's what I mean to say. I get a little distracted and breathy toward the end, as Easton works his way down my neck to trace his tongue over my collarbone. At the same time, his palms slide over the curve of my belly and down to the waistband of my pants, toying with it.

"Frank," he says.

"Now you just *want* to take off your clothes." I nudge him with a foot.

"Uh oh." Easton raises his head, eyes alight. "You got me."

But he shifts back anyway and pushes off his jeans. Which gives me enough time to lever myself upright and pin him underneath me.

"Fine. You want to play hardball?" I kiss his neck. The top of his shoulder. I run my tongue down his abs, toward the V-cut at his groin that always drives me wild. "The right answer was Simon, by the way."

"Simon sounds like an... accountant." Easton's reply skips a fraction too, as my tongue reaches that crease and I nip at the edge of his hipbone.

"What's wrong with accountants? Practical career path, steady money..."

"Come here."

It's impossible to ignore Easton when he talks like that. I sit back up and let him draw me into his lap. He wraps my legs around him, pulls my mouth to his. When we break apart again, I feel the hard press of his cock beneath me, the heave of his chest against mine. When I wrap one hand around the back of his neck, his pulse thunders in tune with mine.

"Whoever our baby is, and whatever their name"— Easton rests a hand on my belly between us—"if they're anything like their mother, they'll be incredible."

My cheeks flush. He can still do that, even after a year plus of marriage. "Well. You do know the right way to distract a lady."

Then I let the flash cards fall to the wayside, as Easton tugs my pants off, tossing them with his in a discarded pile across the room. His hands are both strong and gentle as he braces my hips. He guides his cock to my entrance, and I can tell I'm already wet for him by the way the head of his cock glides back and forth along my slit easily.

"Fuck, Phoebe." His eyes catch mine again.

He eases the tip of his cock inside me and gently draws my hips down, until I'm sitting in his lap, his cock pushing fully inside me. Filling me, stretching me until a pleasant ache spreads through my body. Tingles all the way out to my toes.

"I never get tired of this," he murmurs, mouth inches from mine.

"Who knew married sex wasn't boring at all?" I reply, my laugh breathy. It gets even more so as he grips my hips again. Draws me up and back down along his shaft, so I feel every inch of him.

I wrap my arms around his shoulders and move with him in a gentle, slow rhythm that drives me wild.

"I fucking love you," I breathe and catch him in another kiss, harder this time.

"Trust me," he says, when we pull apart again, both still catching our breath. "Nowhere near as much as I love you."

"Agree to disagree," I fire back, grinning.

Then he drags me against him, thrusting up into me faster, and I lose track of everything else. There's just this. My husband, me, our bodies conjoined. And the new life we created together, about to join our weird yet perfect life.

***

Boom. Done.

LOOKING FOR MORE FUN, fake shenanigans? I have two more romcoms to devour in Kindle Unlimited.

The Playboy's Guide to the Fake Fiancée

The Alphahole's Guide to Marrying Your Enemy

A couple of chapters of The Playboy's Guide are just a scroll away!

***

IF YOU WANT me to send you an email when I have a release, get on my list! JUST CLICK HERE! or go to http://eepurl.com/hV51BH
Email me at piper.marlowe.books@gmail.com
Come to my FACEBOOK PAGE if that's your thing.

THE PLAYBOY'S GUIDE TO THE FAKE FIANCÉE

All I want to do is...well...whatever I want, with whomever I want...preferably without a single string attached. But Dad's secretary keeps calling to make sure I'm not trying to dodge the Friday meeting, where he's gonna dump the Montclaire family business in my lap.

Perfect time for a vaguely familiar woman to pound on my door in the middle of the night.

"Remember me?" she asks. "It's Chloe Davis and you know me from when we were kids. I told my grandmother we were engaged so...would you like to take me to her 85th birthday party? In Florida?"

I would not, but I'll do anything to get out of town for this meeting.

That's how all six feet of me wound up stuffed into the passenger seat of a subcompact, managing snacks, staying in cheap hotel rooms, and sitting in a white Cracker Barrel rocking chair next to the nuttiest, most unpredictable, charming, deliciously sexy woman I've ever avoided responsibility with.

Did I mention she brought her own ring? Of course she did.

Every time I'm sucker enough to think things can't get weirder, they do.

And call me crazy, but this batcrap sandwich of a fake relationship is starting to feel realer than anything I left in New York.

1

DYLAN

I wake up to a thunderstorm.

No. It's a battering ram.

No. Definitely raining. And lightning. And for sure that's a battering ram at my front door. I get out of bed and go to the window, pulling up the blinds to check out the situation.

Williamsburg is the part of Brooklyn with the highest density of places to get cold-pressed juices and nitro-brewed coffee, but this is still New York, where plenty of dangerous people show up on brownstone stoops. I'm not expecting a gang of hardened criminals to knock before entering, but some insufferable hipster high on bath salts isn't out of the question.

But when I look out into the storm, down at the street, I don't see danger. I see a woman.

Not that women can't be dangerous, but in my experience, they're a fun kind of danger. The mystery girl keeps banging her fists on my front door, then she hits the bell a couple times as if she's entitled to come right on in. I must know her. Whatever's going on out there, she means business.

Car must have broken down on Bedford and she figured I was close by. She probably needs a towel. I can't leave her out there to drown, so I head down the stairs.

The banging stops when I hit the lights and unlock the door.

"Can I help you?" I ask when I open up, which is much nicer than "Do you know what time it is?" or guttural snarling.

"Dylan Montclaire?" she says.

I take a quick glance at the girl. She's gotta be in her twenties, rocking a slouchy jeans and hooded sweatshirt aesthetic that suggests she doesn't think about her appearance too much. Her dark hair is in a ponytail, and she apparently didn't bring an umbrella on this little journey. She's soaking wet, tendrils of hair plastered to the sides of her face. A quick glance confirms she's definitely not my type. Not that she's bad-looking. She's cute, in a pouty, nerdy kinda way.

But that means I'm sure I've never slept with her. At least, I'm pretty sure I haven't in the past three months —which rules out a pregnancy test in her pocket. I'm about ninety-seven percent certain about the past six months, maybe—which begs the question, what is she doing on my doorstep in the rain?

Is she here to serve me a subpoena? Or a warrant? I

shouldn't confirm my name. Have I done anything espe-cially terrible the last couple of years? Maybe she was pregnant and had it? Where is it? Is it mine? Like I said, ninety-seven percent sure we've never had sex, but there was that night at Oculus I can barely remember. And the more I stare at her, the more I realize she looks strangely familiar.

"Who's asking?" I say, trying to give myself time to put the pieces together.

"It's me." Then, when I continue my most charming blank stare, she adds, "Chloe Davis."

Ah. Chloe Davis.

"Not a damn clue who that is."

"I need your help."

"Well, actually, I'm not—"

"I need you to marry me," she blurts.

That's definitely a first, and it's definitely that night at Oculus.

"How far along are you?"

"Huh?" She looks baffled by my question.

"No offense, but I want a paternity test. I can't just take your word that I'm the father."

"I'm not pregnant," she says flatly.

Thank God. After my life stops flashing its highlights reel before my eyes, I realize I'm more confused than ever. She doesn't seem to be serving me anything other than an increasingly irritated look, and she's not having a baby. Why the hell is she at my door in the middle of the night?

Well. Either way, it's pouring rain.

"Want to come in?" I step aside, because why not? This is already too goddamn weird.

"Thanks." She wipes her wet feet on the equally wet doormat before entering, like she won't soak my hardwood floors anyway.

I make her stand in the foyer while I grab some towels from the guest bathroom. When I return, she's got her shoes off and is shimmying out of her sodden sweatshirt. She gratefully accepts the towel.

"So. Who are you again?"

"Chloe Davis," she says, as if that should explain everything. She drapes the towel around her shoulders and gazes up at me.

Like I said earlier, she's got a pouty nerd-thing going on that, while not my type, is pretty cute. Even though she looks like a drowned rat at the moment, she's strangely appealing. If you're into drowned rats, of course.

"I'm gonna need more to go on than just the name," I say.

"About the marriage thing. You don't have to actually go through with it." She says this as though it should be reassuring instead of even more confusing.

"How about we start with how we met. Because not to be rude, but it's two in the morning and I have literally no idea what this is all about."

"Why am I not surprised?" she mutters. "Chloe Davis. From the Cape. Remember? Summers '07 to '10?"

That drags me right back to my childhood and all the standard vacation rituals. Bonfires on the beach, pool parties, drinking stolen booze out of a paper bag during the Fourth of July fireworks, stealing my dad's Porsche to race against Chip's dad's Jag. And now, finally, I remember the woman dripping in front of me.

"Got it!" I snap my fingers. "You were the girl with wheels in your shoes."

"They're called Heelys, thank you very much." She gives me a narrow look, like I'm some kind of uncouth monster for not knowing that.

"Look, I remember you now." She's a couple years younger than me. Her family had the summer house next door to mine. Chloe was the kid who always tried to run with the bigger boys, but was just a little too young and gawky to ever click with our crowd. "So hi. Nice to see you again. Been a long time. Please explain to me why this sudden proposal couldn't wait until tomorrow morning."

"I'm on a tight schedule." She keeps giving me that glowering look, but her cheeks are turning red. At least she knows how batshit this is.

"Unless there's a bomb at the base of your skull that detonates at sunrise if you're not engaged, this doesn't make sense."

"Are you thinking *Escape from New York* style bomb?" She looks really serious about this question. "Or more of a *Suicide Squad* thing?"

I appreciate her taste in movies, but I don't need this conversation to go any farther down the rabbit hole of weird. "You got five seconds to convince me not to call you an Uber."

"Fine! I need to get pretend-married for my grandmother."

I nod, waiting for her to make that make sense. She doesn't.

"Gonna need more," I say.

"For some reason, I thought this would be easier," she mutters. "Look. My grandmother is Geraldine Davis. Like 'former Park Avenue powerhouse socialite, current queen of Florida' Geraldine Davis. She's the kind of woman who thinks whiskey highballs are a brunch staple. She may have been involved with half of the Rat Pack in their Vegas days, all at the same time. Do you understand what I'm saying?"

"Your grandma is fun to party with. Still don't see where I come in."

Chloe rolls her eyes. "Point is, my grandma doesn't understand why her granddaughter wants to spend her most 'fertile years' as a kindergarten teacher raising other people's children. She's onboard with certain parts of women's lib, particularly the sexual revolution." Chloe shudders a bit at placing the words "grandma" and "sexual" in the same sentence, and I'm right there with her. "But when it comes to family, she's a total Stepford Wife. I'm only twenty-four, and she's already giving me shit about my biological clock."

I put the pieces together. "Let me guess. You told her you were engaged to get her off your ass."

"Yes."

"And she wants to meet this poor guy."

"Yes." She seems impressed with my accuracy.

Gotta admit, I'm pretty impressed myself. I go for two. "And you don't have a nice gay friend who wants to try?"

"I can't be engaged to just anyone." Chloe crosses her arms and cocks her hip, and even though she's, like, five-two and a hundred pounds literally soaking wet, there's some real take-charge, alpha fire in her eyes. Maybe not my type, but it is sort of hot. "Last month, we were getting into it again and I told her I was engaged to you. *The* Dylan Montclaire. It was the first time in years I heard her sound that happy."

Not to be too narcissistic, but I can see why. If Grams is a former New York socialite, she'll know all about the Montclaires. The family business is booming, and I've been groomed for leadership from the moment I could count the twenties the Tooth Fairy left under my pillow. I'm the sort any social climber worth her margarita salt wants in the family gene pool.

"You don't need my permission to lie about this, if that's what you're asking."

"Here's the problem. Grandma's eighty-fifth birthday is coming up soon."

"Eighty-five? She's got stamina." Which flashes me back to the sexual revolution bit, and I shake off the images.

"She's having a giant blow-out bash down in Florida."

Finally, it all clicks. What she's doing here. What she's asking. Why she had to come at me guns blazing in the middle of the night, before she convinced herself it was a ridiculous idea.

"Oh. Oh no." I put up my hands like a guy fending off a hug from a sweaty friend, but this girl's a herd of cattle and she plows right on ahead.

"The whole family will be there. It's a lot of people. We breed like rabbits. Very rich, semi-alcoholic rabbits. She already asked about you on a group call and I said you were coming. If I show up without you, Grandma's gonna put it all together. I'll be humiliated in front of everyone."

"No, you won't. Because 'everyone' includes me, and I won't be there."

"Her party's next week." Chloe barrels ahead, knowing she's about to lose me. "I can't show up alone."

"Then hire a male escort and pass him off as me," I snap. This is too easy. "Everyone knows what you look like! My parents and my sisters and my grandmother all spent summers at our house on the Cape, and everyone else can just Google you! You're not exactly low-profile."

Yeah. Being a semi-playboy Fortune 500 scion in the Internet era makes life extra fascinating.

"Tell them it's Dylan Montclaire without the 'e' at the end. Just some random Dylan who coaches finger painting or whatever teachers do these days."

"I know how crazy this looks and sounds," she says.

"Well, actually it doesn't *sound* crazy."

"Really?"

"It's fucking nuts."

"I can make it worth your while." She slips a pair of

Warby Parker glasses out of her jeans pocket and slides them onto her face. It is the opposite of a seductive move, so I'm not sure what she's getting at. "The party's down in Florida, like I said. At the Villages. You know it?"

"The retirement community?" I drawl.

"Oooh, the Villages? Sounds baller!"

Chloe and I turn toward the tall, voluptuous woman at the top of the stairs of my brownstone, a huge smile on her face. Lacey Simpson—good, solid friend plus all the perks—struts down in her lace panties and bra without a care in the damn world. That cheerful, easy-going attitude is one of the reasons I like sleeping with her. Her dynamite body and insane sex drive also help.

If I'm expecting Chloe to be shocked by my happy hookup walking around almost in the nude, turns out I'm wrong. Chloe doesn't flush or look away. Okay, so the nerd girl's not a prude. She seemed like the buttoned-up type, but turns out I was wrong.

"Right? Trust me, my grandmother knows how to throw a mean party," Chloe says in all earnestness. What a sentence.

"Florida means Orlando," Lacey says. "Orlando means Disney World. If you two get hitched, you can get the newlywed discount!" She sounds excited by the idea.

Chloe's whole face lights up and she snaps her fingers. "See? That's a great plan!"

I do not need a discount to anything, particularly Disney World. I've got plenty of cash and too much taste for this.

"I'm guessing you heard everything?" I ask Lacey.

She sweeps past me and into the living room, where she plucks at the couch cushions. Finally, she nabs something with a triumphant "aha!" and slides into it. Right, her skirt.

Not sure where her top is. Or at least one of her shoes. We got down to business as soon as we came home.

"I heard everything. You two knew each other as kids. She needs a date; you need a life. It's perfect!" Lacey snatches one of her stilettos, then goes hunting for the other. Ah, shit. Looks like she's prepping to leave, and I was hoping for a round two or three before she headed back to the Upper West Side.

"You said you'd make it worth my while?" I turn back to Chloe, a headache forming behind my eyes. "Okay. What's in this for me?"

"Uh. A vacation, of course!" This girl really is flying by the seat of her pants, and she knows it. "A few days of sun and relaxation, all expenses paid."

"Thanks, but I don't need to sponge off a kindergarten teacher." I'm kind of insulted she even offered.

"Then just the sun and relaxation part. Plus, you'll get to attend one of Geraldine Davis's birthday bashes. They're legendary, and not just among the geriatrics driving golf carts."

"Do it, Dylan." Lacey pokes her head back into the hallway as she slides on her top. With every button she does up, my mood plummets. "This sounds like too much fun."

"Whose side are you on?" I ask.

"The side of good times. Duh." Lacey tosses her ombre-d curls over her shoulder as she puts in one earring. She pauses, then goes looking for the other one.

"Look. I'm sorry, but I can't take off time for this." Despite the current madness, I don't want to be a dick to Chloe. I'm remembering her more and more now. She was a nice kid and she seems like she grew into a nice person. It's just that I've never been nice. "Apologies, Heely Girl, but I have too much going on."

"Nooooo, he does not," Lacey calls from the kitchen.

"Yes. I do," I shout back.

She returns, clasping a bracelet as she does. "Dylan, did you forget what's happening next week?" Lacey arches a perfectly plucked brow. "It's the big meeting with dear ol' Daddy-sensei."

Oh, shit. She's right. My father's been trying to hand off the company's reins to me for almost three years now, and I've been desperate to stay away from this conversation. Just because I can wear suits and attend meetings like a boss doesn't mean it's what I want for the rest of my life. But when you're a Montclaire, you're given the Spider-Man talk when you're six years old—with great power comes great responsibility. I got to grow up privileged because of the family business, and that means I need to devote my life to it. According to my father, that is.

This time, he's planning to force my hand. He wants me to take my place at last, the prodigal son of Fifth Avenue.

Just thinking about that meeting makes my

sphincter clench. Lacey's a vendor rep for the family company, meaning she knows all about this.

"If you've got a meeting you want to avoid, Florida's the perfect place to go," Chloe says. She flashes a thumbs-up to Lacey, who beams. What is this, some girl conspiracy between them?

"Seriously, best possible idea right now," Lacey says. To Chloe, she continues. "Dylan is *not* looking to take his place at the head of the table, if you know what I mean."

"Oh yeah. I definitely do," Chloe says. "Trust me, failing to meet family expectations is my thing."

"Are the two of you finished?" I glare at Lacey, the damn sexy traitor. "Lace, why don't *you* just go with her?"

"I can't pretend to be you. I don't have the jaw angularity," Lacey says.

"I think we can help each other out." Chloe looks damned pleased, because she thinks she sees the way to get around me. After all, spoiled rich guy running from the family yoke? Tale as old as time.

"There is no us. No 'we,' no 'help,' no 'each other.' Got it?" I snap.

I can't stop my increasingly shit mood. Lacey's already sliding into her coat, looking more than ready to skip out.

Chloe huffs. "Is he always like this?" she asks Lacey.

"Normally he's pretty chill after he gets laid. This must be an off night." Lacey shrugs, then snatches her purse from the hall table. "Here. Leave him your number."

She lays a receipt and a pen down next to the lamp.

"Oooh, good idea." Chloe snatches the pen and writes out her contact information. Apparently neither of them is going to listen to me.

"Hey. Hey! I'm not doing this. Do you hear me?"

"Your father won't mind you skipping town to meet your future in-laws. Trust me," Chloe says.

"I don't! I do not trust you." Incredulous, I watch her hand the pen back to Lacey as Chloe taps the receipt.

"Call me when you change your mind," Chloe says.

"That will be exactly never." I can't believe I'm having this surreal conversation at two thirty in the morning.

"Not to be a prude," Chloe says to Lacey, "but it's kind of inappropriate for my fiancé to have half-naked girls over at his apartment."

Both of them look like they're about to crack up. Fuck me.

"You're so right. Want to split a ride back?" Lacey asks Chloe as she belts her coat. Oh *come on.* "Where are you headed?"

"Astoria." Chloe slips back into her sneakers. Good, at least she's going.

"Hm. Opposite direction."

"Oh, don't worry. I always take the train after dark. Or I walk."

"To Queens?" Lacey sounds incredulous. Enough of this.

"You. Don't go." I point at Lacey, then Chloe. "You. Goodbye."

"Your fiancé's very rude," Lacey whispers.

Chloe sighs. "Relationships never go the way you picture them."

She towels off her hair one more time while Lacey glances at her phone. She is actually calling a car. I can't believe this.

"Look, my number's just there." Chloe glances at the receipt again. "Whenever you change your mind, you know where to find me."

"God. You really are as stubborn as I remember."

Hell on Wheels, that's what we called her.

"So that's a yes?" Chloe says.

I respond by opening the door. At least the rain has lessened over the last fifteen minutes. I hand Chloe her wet sweatshirt, then help her over my threshold and back out into the storm.

"So long, Heely Girl," I say. "Good luck with your grandma. Sorry I couldn't help."

"Hey!" Chloe's look of exasperated surprise is the last thing I see as I shut the door between us.

After a minute, I hear a tapping behind me. One of Lacey's stiletto-d feet clicks in irritation. She crosses her arms and narrows her eyes.

"You are *so* not getting laid again tonight, pal," she says.

Figures.

2

CHLOE

I'M ON THE F TRAIN AT SIX THIRTY IN THE MORNING, AND I'M about to pass out after a crushing lack of sleep. I slump against the pole in the middle of the car, eyes fluttering shut. The teenagers on their way to school shoot me a sympathetic look, while the other commuting adults stare at their phones. At least it's quiet in here right now. If a Mariachi band comes aboard, I'll probably die.

Maybe that'd be a blessing. I got home at three thirty last night after walking through a rainstorm. I took a blow dryer to my hair and should've immediately gone to bed. Hey, two hours of sleep is better than none. But after that epic humiliation at Dylan's, I knew I couldn't close my eyes. I ended up digging into a pint of Dulce de Leche Haagen Dazs while watching *Roman Holiday* with Audrey Hepburn and trying not to cry.

Which, come to think of it, is how I spend most Saturday nights. I'm beyond pathetic.

After all, a non-pathetic person doesn't show up on an acquaintance's doorstep at two in the morning to ask him to fake-marry her. A non-pathetic person doesn't lie to her grandma about being engaged.

But you know what a non-pathetic person *would* do? Pick herself up, dust herself off, and try to come up with another plan to lie about her love life.

My new plan does not require Dylan Montclaire. Don't get me wrong, he'd be the perfect fake fiancé. After all, he's still really, really handsome, maybe even more than I remember from when I was a kid. I almost blacked out when he answered the door without a shirt on, looking like the hottest and surliest underwear model in history.

Honestly, when I realized how much perfection he managed to exhibit in one tightly-wrapped package, my plan didn't make much sense. How was I supposed to show up with a god on my arm and act like we fit together? I think I'm pretty enough, but pretty enough isn't enough when the man is that, well, pretty. People date and marry the people who fit in their lives. A regular girl with a ponytail and a closet full of sweatshirts isn't Dylan Montclaire's type. He's the kind of guy you'd pair with a woman like Lacey—tall, voluptuous, and elegantly put-together. Lacey was cool, so it's not a dig at her. It's a dig at me for thinking I could ever entice a guy like Dylan.

I shake my head and tell myself to stop all these

negative thoughts. When the kids in my class make fun of each other or feel down about themselves, I firmly tell them that everyone is beautiful and brilliant in their own special way, and we should all respect that about one another. I can't tell them that if I don't take my own advice.

The plan is to make Grandma happy in her last months on this earth, and I'll do that or die trying No matter what. Even if I have to hire a male escort, or pretend Dylan was killed in a freak yachting accident. I'll do what it takes to make my grandma happy.

After another couple of transfers, I'm finally walking down the street to my school in the Bronx. I smile when I see all the kids racing up the steps to enter the building, giggling and shrieking about how they can't wait for summer. School's set to end in a few weeks. Then I can get started on my sexy summer plans, which involve adopting a cat and organizing my bookshelf by color. It'll be a summer to remember.

My phone buzzes, and for a crazy moment I think it's Dylan calling me to say he's changed his mind and, yes, he'd love to come to Florida and hold my hand in front of my whole family, but caller ID says it's my older sister, Anna. Oh well. I'm always happy to hear from her.

"Hey! I'm about to head into school. What's up?"

"You're starting work, I'm just about done. Ugh, I'm dead on my feet. Kimi didn't show at Saudade, so I ended up pulling a double shift. You would not believe how many Appletinis German businessmen drink."

My sister is one of the hottest bartenders at one of

the hottest clubs in the Meatpacking District. I frown. "Anna, it's almost eight in the morning. Saudade closes at four. How are you just getting home?"

"German businessmen who like Appletinis also like bringing American girls to their fancy hotel rooms." I can hear her smug satisfaction over the phone. "Want me to make a joke about Germans and their enormous sausages, or is that too cliché for this early in the morning?"

My sister and I are polar opposites. I told her once that she's the Arctic to my Antarctic, then told her I had to be Antarctica because I love penguins and am scared of polar bears. She told me that was both sad and adorable at the same time.

"Anyway, I got your text last night but couldn't call until now. What's up?"

Right, time to humiliate myself about Dylan Montclaire some more. At least I know Anna won't laugh in my face. She'll wait until we're off the phone.

"Um, was it you who told me about that duke who asked you to marry him while you were stuck on his private jet?"

"Lawrence. He was an earl actually."

"He got you a ring, right?"

"Yes. Where are you going with this?"

"Do you still have it?"

Anna pauses. "Do we have to play Twenty Questions, or can I know what's going on?"

I sigh. "Remember Dylan Montclaire from Cape Cod?"

That's how I end up telling Anna about my trek out to Brooklyn, getting caught in the rainstorm, showing up on Dylan's doorstep in the early morning, him without a shirt on, him shoving me out the door with a firm no. I tell her about my lie to Grandma and my need to let her die clutching the belief that I've snagged a hot billionaire. My sister is trying hard not to laugh at me, I can tell.

"Chloe. You are the sweetest, weirdest sister anyone could ask for."

"Thanks. Ugh, I just need to figure out a way to convince Grams I'm engaged to Dylan without having to actually produce Dylan. That should be easy, right? It's so simple to doctor images with Photoshop these days, I'm sure I can insert him into a few pictures. Like when we went to the aquarium? Or that last Halloween party?"

"Since we went as the twin girls from *The Shining*, I bet it'll be hard to insert Dylan in my place, but I'm sure he looks good in a blue dress and a bow." Anna chuckles. She's the only member of my family who thinks my kookiness is a feature, not a bug, and I love her for it.

"I can figure this out! I know I can. I'm hoping that if I show up with a couple of pictures and a nice engagement ring on my finger, Grams won't ask too many questions. I can say that Dylan's busy back in New York, right? Doing billionaire things at his business?"

"If you're going to pull a fast one on Grams, my first advice is to figure out what Dylan's actual title at his job is," Anna teases. "'Billionaire things' is cool-sounding on a resume, but not very specific."

"Ah, shoot, you're right." The warning bell goes off,

letting us know we've got five minutes before the school day begins. I need to get to the kindergarten room and set up the finger painting station. Since it's almost summer, I'm having the kids make starfish with their hands.

"Do you think I can do this? Honestly?"

"Honestly? No, I'm sorry. I think this is going to be an epic disaster." Anna's not being mean, just truthful. Truth hurts sometimes. "On the bright side, I think it'll be a fun disaster."

"Look, I know this can't fool anyone else in the family, but you know Grams. She always sees what she wants to see. If I can make her final birthday party a big success, that's all I need."

"Yeah." Anna sounds a little sad. We all are, considering this is the last time we can gather to celebrate Geraldine Davis. She may be a handful, but she's the most alive person I've ever met. "I get it. I want to make her happy too. It's why I keep pretending I'm still in medical school."

The only reason Grams doesn't give Anna a hard time about getting married is because she thinks Anna's on the fast track to being Dr. Davis. If she knew my older sister is a twenty-seven-year-old bartender, she'd lose her mind and her dentures.

"So. Do you have the earl's ring? And can I borrow it?"

"Before I answer that, let me ask this. Do you think it might be better to just come clean to Grams? I mean, you're only twenty-four. It's normal these days to be that age and not have a partner."

"I can't." The answer is immediate. Anna doesn't know how excited our grandmother was when I told her about Dylan and me. This lie has taken on a life of its own, and right now, I'm doing frantic CPR while it flat-lines on the table. Speaking of CPR... "If Grams finds out I told such a whopper of a lie, her heart might give out from the shock. I can't take that risk."

"Okay. Well, in that case, yes, I have the ring and..." She pauses for maximum dramatic buildup. "You can borrow it. It's an honest-to-God real Tiffany engagement ring."

Thank God I wasn't drinking anything just then, or I'd have spit it all over the sidewalk and the last children rushing to get to class on time.

"You sure get a lot done with three dates."

"If by 'dates' you mean 'had sex with,' then yeah. He was nice enough but could only find my clit, like, fifty percent of the time, which is just a deal-breaker for me. I need to be satisfied if I'm going to be with somebody in the long term."

My jaw has dropped open by now. My sister is apparently extremely good at the sex, and I wince just thinking that sentence. Even though I'm sure it's super accurate.

"And he won't find out and send the English army after me or something?"

"I tried to get him to take the ring back, but he was crying and everything and it got real uncomfortable real fast. He told me to keep it, then said he was going back to his estate to be depressed for the rest of his life. I'm sure he'll find a nice girl in the countryside or whatever. Anyway, it's one hundred percent mine and now I have the literal perfect engagement ring for you."

"Thank you so much, Anna. I knew you'd come through for me."

"Just to be, like, very clear, I need it back in good condition. Diamonds are a girl's best friend, and that one could be a down payment on a nice Midtown condo someday."

My sister is very sweet and also very mercenary. It's something else I love about her.

"I'll keep it safe, I promise. You're the best. Okay, love you. Bye."

We hang up and I grin as I head to my classroom, ready to put together a finger-painting station in record time. Even if I can't have Dylan, I can have an engagement ring worthy of my lie. Grams will be thrilled, which is all that matters now.

Though I can't help wishing I had the man to go with the ring.

GET **The Playboy's Guide to the Fake Fiancée** FREE in Kindle Unlimited!

ROMCOMS BY PIPER MARLOWE

The Billionaire's Guide to the Marriage Deal

Phoebe isn't exactly my type, which is the plan--easy to marry, easy to leave.

Some would call it a marriage of convenience. So why can't I stop imagining something more real with my fake wife?

The Playboy's Guide to the Fake Fiancée

How did all six feet of me wind up stuffed into the passenger seat of a subcompact with the nuttiest, sexiest woman I've ever met?

This fake relationship is starting to feel realer than anything I left in New York.

The Alphahole's Guide to Marrying Your Enemy

I wouldn't date Sydney Taylor if she was the last woman on earth, which is why—if I marry her—my mother will believe it's real.

After a hate-boink or two...I'm definitely going to walk away. Really.